FRODE - IRON AGE DETECTIVE
RETRIBUTION

Copyright © 2023 by Geoff Bunn

All rights reserved. This book or any portion thereof may not be reproduced or used in any manner whatsoever without the express written permission of the publisher except for the use of brief quotations in a book review or scholarly journal.

First Printing: 2023
ISBN: 9798844559242

FRODE -
IRON AGE DETECTIVE

RETRIBUTION

Geoff Bunn

It was a time of DEATH *and dying.*

But the people were not afraid to die, they did not live in fear like children scared of the dark.

What did matter to them, to all of them, was HOW *they died.*

And where there were any doubts about a death, then they called upon the skills of a VERIFIER - *not exactly a 'detective', but the closest thing they had...*

1

No longer summer nor yet winter, the night was still, calm and quiet. Untroubled. People slept. And they slept soundly. Dogs, chickens, geese all silent. The whole world at rest. Perhaps only cats crept out, here and there, craftily, stealthily, hunting for their midnight prey.

It was a time of peace. A good time.

Who, then, could have reason to stir on such a gentle night? Only those who found torment in their deepest sleep, in their dreams, in their nightmares...

"No! No! There are screams. Horrible screams all around me. All around the clearing.

"No, no. No! The village. My village. It's on fire!

"Men, appearing from every direction. Men, drawn swords, blood on the tips of their blades. Who are they? Don't know them. Don't know them. Run. Run. Run. No! Stop, I must go back, I must go back and help the others. Go back and find my own sword. Fight.

"Turn this way, turn that.

"Turn, turn, turn.

"But I can't find my home. I can't find my own home!

"A sword, sharp edged, lethal, swings at me. Flashing past my face. It misses me. So close. But I fall over. Helpless I'm now on my back. The same sword is raised up above me, I can see it, high in the air above me, it is going to kill me, that man is going to kill me. This is my death!"

"Per, wake up!"

"He drops the blade. Falls forward. He lands on top of me. His weight, great weight, I cannot breathe.

"Screams. More screams.

"I pull myself out from beneath the body.

"There is fire all around now. Fire. Homes burning. People being killed. Smoke everywhere. I pick myself up and run, and run, and run. Run until I can breathe no more. Until I can breathe no more. Help, help! HELP!"

"Per!"

"I keep moving. I hear my name called. Someone is calling me. Shaking me.

"I am in the forest. Deep snow. Somehow I manage to keep moving, moving away from the horror behind me. The village, my village, sacked, burned, murdered. I cannot help them".

"Per, wake up! Wake up! It is me, Suli. Wake up. You are having a bad dream".

"Eyes blurred, unsure of where I am, there is no smell of burning, there are no screams. None. Nothing. None except for my own. My own screams which have now stopped as I wake. As I wake... As I wake...

"Where am I?

"I am lying down.

"Where am I?

"I am in my bed. In my bed. I am in my own bed. Here. I am here. I am safe. At home. I am at home."

"Per? Wake up!"

"Uhh", said Per. Waking. Finally waking enough to speak. "Uh... what? Oh... yes. Yes, you are right. I am dreaming".

Suli, young, strong, blonde haired, blue eyed, leant over the older man. Then, seeing that Per was now awake, he stepped back. Relieved somewhat. "It was only a dream", said Suli.

Per sat up in his bed, what passed for a bed in the late Iron Age, a deep, tidily piled mattress of straw, kept in place with wooden boards at either side and at both ends. He looked around. An expression of shock on his face. The horror fading. Being replaced by a visible sense of relief. Yes, he was in his own home. Home and sitting up in bed.

"Was it that same dream, again?" said Suli, his voice quiet, calm, almost soft. It was, after all, the dead of night.

Per nodded his head. "Yes". He cleared his throat. Dry as it was from the disturbed sleep, the fear, the nightmare. "Yes, yes it was the same one. Horrible".

Suli sat down on a rough wooden bench which, during the daytime, was often used as a low table.

"Tell me about it, then", said Suli. "Was it exactly the same? Was it in the snow, again?"

It was not a dream, it was not even a nightmare. It was a recollection, a vivid flashback to a brutal day, ten, twelve or more years beforehand. A memory. A trauma. An all too real event which Per had once lived through and somehow survived. And which, in troubled sleep, he often relived. But he would not tell Suli that. He would not let on that the 'dream' was real. He had never told anybody about it. The fact that his recurring nightmare was something he had actually experienced. No. Nor would he ever do so. At least, such was the promise he had always made to himself.

"It might help you to understand it, or to stop dreaming it if you tell me all about it." said Suli.

Per nodded his head. Swung his shortened body off the 'bed' and sat, for a moment, eyes staring fixedly down at his small feet.

Per had told Suli all about the 'dream' before. But it had not gone away. It had not helped. Not really. But now? It was the middle of the night, the world outside their grimy hut was silent, and Per could not find it within himself to go back to sleep. Not back to that world. No. In case he found himself back in that same place. Pursued by men with swords tipped in blood. The blood of neighbours, the blood of friends, the blood of family.

"I will tell you", said Per, standing up. "Yes. But first, I need a drink".

Per was a dwarf. Offensively, men and women like Per were often called midgets. Some, for reasons known only to themselves, even found little people, such as Per, to be comical by virtue of their smaller size. Something to ridicule. And Per had heard plenty of that in his time, often feeling hurt by it in his youth. But then, with the murderous sacking of his home village, and as the years had slowly gone by, he had long ceased taking offence at the small mindedness of such folk. Life, both horribly and, more simply, through the crude passage of time, had shown him that other things mattered far more than such insults.

"I think we finished the last of the beer", said Suli apologetically. "There is perhaps only a little sour milk left, now".

Per sighed. This was not really a time for milk. Sour or otherwise.

"Go back to bed", urged Suli. "We have a lot of work tomorrow and it is late".

"I will", said Per. "I will, but first I must take something for my mouth. It feels so dry".

He peered into a number of wooden bowls, one after the other, bowls which had been set to one side the evening before, after eating, for rinsing out. In the last of them there were a few remnants of stew, even a piece of coarse bread. Torn but unbitten. He wiped the bread around in the stew, and then ate it, slowly, thoughtfully.

Thanks to remarkable handicraft skills, Per had become widely known and well-respected throughout this, his adopted town, his adopted region. He sculpted, crafted, from bone, but sometimes from other materials such as amber or semi-precious stones, the most intricate and exquisite figurines. Horses, dogs, mystical animals, gods but, mainly, people. Faces and miniature bodies, men, women and children. Giving them all such a sense of life, a feeling of animation, of actual existence, that people were often quite mesmerised by them.

What were the figurines for? It depended. For religious or spiritual ends. For decoration. Even for memory to help keep the face of a lost partner alive. All sorts of reasons. Per rarely asked, for it was not his business to know.

And his hut, both his home and workshop, and no larger than a stable for one horse, reflected his trade. Though in no sense did it reflect his success. There were shavings of bone, and wood, all over the floor. Small tools, incredibly delicate, scattered here and there. A dark, old and oil stained wooden bench, on which he toiled. Tiny figures, unfinished, but in progress. A few polished pieces, waiting for the people who had ordered them to call and collect. And very little sign of any wealth, few if any creature comforts.

But Per did not care about such things. He wouldn't have used them, nor even noticed them, had they been in his hut. His day consisted of waking, food, a few simple ablutions and then work. Carving, filing, pinching, nicking, sharpening, shaping, creating. Every day the same. Somehow that endless toil offering him the escape he needed from the nightmare of that village, the horrors of that night, all those years ago.

The last of the remnants of bread and stew finished, Per stood and walked back to his bed.

Suli, with nowhere better to sleep than on the floor, the home too small, the space too crowded, for him to have a permanent bed like Per, had piled up some straw and he now lay upon it, pulling more of the stuff over himself to help keep him warm and, by so doing, in effect, almost disappearing from sight.

"Are you asleep already?"

"No", replied Suli. "I want to hear about your dream".

Per sniffed. Then swung himself up and into his own 'mattress' of straw.

Suli was a good lad. Still only young, somewhat less than twenty years old and always willing to work, always prepared to help. Quite the opposite of Per, Suli was a typical Scandinavian in many ways – being tall, blonde and blue eyed. Also unlike Per, Suli had been born down here, in the far south of the land. His own harsh misfortunate, early in life, had been to be lose his family to disease, mother and father, no brothers or sisters, he had been orphaned perhaps ten or twelve years beforehand. Had his family been larger, had they lived in a village or some sort of community, settled, he may still have fared well, despite that loss. But his family had been isolated, one small home, and no such social network existed for him, nor indeed a family of any kind. Suli once orphaned, was abandoned and would have died.

It happened.

These were hard times.

But the little boy had been found, more or less starving, and brought to the town where Per, in his turn, having seen some promise in the boy as time passed, had agreed to teach him his own craft, as best he could.

And Suli could already make figurines. Fine handiwork, too. Though still, needless to say, showing none of the prowess of his 'master'.

"Well... the dream, this dream, the one I keep having, is set in winter. A winter where the snow has arrived early. Deep and early. Very early", began Per, lying on his back, looking up at the dark underside of the thatched roof, beneath which they slept every night, a dark underside where nothing really could now be seen, apart from vague impressions of the thatch itself and the rough hewn timbers which formed the framework for the roof. "And, because of that, by the middle of winter, the winter proper, all across the region, in every home, in every village, people are struggling and food is very short".

Per did not want to close his eyes as he spoke, in case the whole thing would once more become a vivid and stark reality.

"Like the winter we had here, you mean, a few years back?"

"No", said Per. "No. This one was much worse than that. The snow so much deeper, and it came sooner, and stayed for longer. And the hunger was far, far greater".

"Were crops lost, too?" Suli asked the question. Losing crops, to harsh weather, was probably the greatest natural danger of the time.

"Yes", said Per. "Or, at least, yes, I mean in my dream, yes, I think so".

"The winter came so early then".

"Yes".

"And then what happened?"

Per described it, the sacking, whilst keeping the details as few as possible, the very scenes he had once witnessed and still so often recalled: the strangers, the killing, the terror. The faces of those men. Or, at least, of some of them. How could he ever forget those?

Then he described how, somehow, he had managed to escape. Struggling through the deep snow into the harsh and endless dark forest. On and on. All the time fearing and expecting to feel, an arrow in his back, or a sword, or a blow from a heavy blunt weapon of some kind.

Yet none such came.

He had gone on, and on, eventually collapsing into the snow, believing for all the world that he would die that very night, of cold, of hunger or of fear, if nothing else. Heart pounding, ready to burst.

"And is that where I wake you up?" said Suli.

Per, very gently, nodded his head. In truth the moment he called out, the moment Suli woke him, probably varied. There were lots of moments where he cried out.

"It sounds horrible", said Suli, his voice soft, almost sleepy. "And so real. Is it truly only a dream you are describing?"

Per frowned. Not that Suli could see his doing so. "Yes", he said. "Yes. It's just a dream".

A dream, Per hoped, he would not encounter again this night as sleep came back to his tired mind and heavy eyes.

"No wonder it disturbs you so", said Suli. "I am glad I don't have such nightmares".

But Per made no reply. Because he had already, finally, fallen asleep again.

*

The location? To Per and Suli, their lives were now being lived in Ostmar, a large market town with a static population of more than two thousand souls. On certain days, at certain times of the year, that population would grow to almost five thousand and perhaps even more than that as both trade and traders came to call. And there were no other towns of a comparable size within any sort of readily achievable distance. In fact, to many who lived in Ostmar, their town was, or it felt as if it was, the only large settlement in the world. More than that? To them, and to the folk with whom they shared their world, location did not matter, it was simply not important.

But to us? Per and Suli lived in what we know today as Sweden. Southern Sweden to be exact, Ostmar being located a few miles to the North West of where the city of Lund stands today.

And the date? Well, the exact date was not known. Not precisely. Once again, to Per, Suli and everyone else who lived in Ostmar, it was simply autumn, spring or summer, winter before the snow, or winter during the snow, festivals and trading days, or not, and more than any of that, they did not need to know nor did they care.

In fact, it was the year 700 AD.

More or less.

The last decades of the Swedish Iron Age.

The Vendel Period.

Only one hundred years before the emergence of the people we know as Viking.

People often imagine that the Iron Age was a time of rudimentary clothes, made of fur or animal skins, a time of cave dwelling with humanity in possession of no great skills other than the ability to make spears and hunt game. But that was life in the Stone Age. (Or, at least, that was how the Stone Age may have been). By the time of the Iron Age, certainly the late Iron Age, life was very, very different to that.

For a start, by 700 AD, the Romans had already come and gone. And although they'd had only limited direct contact with Scandinavia, there had been enough, and more than enough, for many aspects of Roman life to make an impact on the day to day lives of men like Per and Suli. Tools, weapons, jewellery, housing, food, drink and more besides had changed, advanced, altered rapidly in the preceding centuries. Gold, for instance, had made its way into Scandinavia in pretty substantial amounts during the Roman years, and people had, in some respects, gotten accustomed to it. Recent decades, however, had seen gold become more and more sparse and more and more valuable, with bronze being used instead for things like coinage and intricate jewellery.

But over and above that, even without Roman influence, the indigenous people themselves had made great progress in the fields of metalworking, leather work, clothing, pottery and a lot more besides.

Yes, this was still the Iron Age, but it was nearing the end of that period and so life, in very many respects, would have been quite similar to – and immediately recognisable by the inhabitants of – life in England in, say, the 1400s. And it was probably only in respect of culture, the shape of society, the beliefs of society, that things differed substantially from those later times.

In short, the Vendel Period, 700 AD, was the late Iron Age and life *was* hard. But it was also very far removed from those distant days of cave-dwelling and stone headed axes.

*

The Baltic sea is a tideless sea.

Where the wild shores of England and Ireland may see a twice daily rise and fall of several metres, the waters of the Baltic scarcely move. A sandcastle built today, on the fine white beaches of southern Sweden, will still be there tomorrow. And, quite possibly, for many months to come.

But none of that is to say that the Baltic sea is a safe sea, a placid or calm water, more akin to a pond than an ocean, because it is no such thing: on the right kind of day, even though they make scant progress across the beach, the waves of the Baltic can still be huge. Crashing ashore, splendidly, with an almost clockwork monotony. And once in the water, those same waves, combined with powerful tows or undercurrents can easily pull any unsuspecting soul deeper into the sea. Deeper, further out, further and beyond their depth. So dangerous are these surges, in fact, that today there is a general rule for those who want to swim in the Baltic – walk out, swim back. For to do otherwise, is to risk your own life.

Frode had seen men drown, in just such a manner.

Once, a long time ago, attempting to recover their upturned boat - in practice little more than a very basic canoe, used for fishing inshore - two men had returned to the sea, arms stretching trying to reach their craft, strong bodies gradually getting into deeper water, those on the shore calling them back. Those calls increased. But it was already too late. Below the angrily agitated surface of that particular day, a strong current pulled. And pulled. And within only a few metres of the shore, both men were suddenly, awfully, lost. The space they had occupied becoming clear water. Innocent reflection of the sunlight. A wave then rising and falling across that same patch of sea, leaving a flat calm behind it. For all the world it looked just as if nobody had ever been there.

Those on safe dry land, watched, called, waited, helplessly. But nothing could be done. And, as far as Frode knew, neither body had ever been found. Those deep undercurrents could have taken them miles out to sea, and finally deposited them again... who knew where.

So yes, tideless or not, the Baltic was still a very dangerous sea.

Frode shuddered.

Today was also a fine sunlit day. Exactly as it had been all those years ago. And the sea, though not wild, was still, somehow, strangely reminiscent of that day. And so, out there, he assumed, beneath the wavelets, with their white breaking tops, those same sinister forces still sucked and pulled. Sucked and pulled.

But this was not a day to think about such things.

No.

And he made a conscious attempt to turn his back on the water and to return to his work. Bending over to scour great thick clumps of dark green seaweed. Searching in amongst it, freshly washed ashore as it had been, for even the tiniest nuggets of amber. The beautiful, waxy, fossilised tree resin from which he earned a living, trading the stuff all across what would eventually become southern Sweden.

Frode, himself, had been born a long way to the north of where he now spent his time and earned his livelihood. But back there, in the deep dark forests, where life was even harder, he had enemies who would have paid handsomely to lay their hands upon him. So he was content enough, and more than content, to live and wander throughout these southern realms.

"Ah! Now *that* is a beautiful piece", he said out loud, though he was talking to himself, as there was nobody else around. Probably not even for several miles.

And with those words, he crouched down low, bent forward and brushed thick strands of greasy seaweed aside to reveal a nugget of amber the size of a man's clenched fist.

His timing, however, could not have been worse.

For at that very moment, one of the wilder, larger, splashier waves broke. And it broke right above him.

"Nooooo". Frode leapt up, instinctively, up and away from the water's edge. Already soaked. Soaked and laughing. The sun shone brightly, and it was a warm sort of day, albeit early in autumn, and he would dry off soon enough.

He looked back down at the place where the nugget was... or, rather, where it had been.

But it was gone. The wave, the sea, had claimed it back.

"Oh no. Damn it!"

He searched for a while, in and around the same spot, but there was no sign of the thing.

Amber floats. But it also gets pulled under a wave, spun around, twisted all over the place, yanked down deep, before another flourish of water will bring it back to the surface and deposit it somewhere else.

"I've lost it".

A smaller piece of amber, no bigger than the tip of a thumb, caught his eye and, glad of something rather than nothing, Frode smiled, made the Iron Age equivalent of a cross upon himself, and scooped the thing up, before another large wave smashed on the very same place.

"You've been generous", said Frode, directing his words at the sea, or the gods of the sea, or nature, or whatever it was that was out there. "And for that I thankyou"

Perhaps there was nothing at all out there. Frode could never, quite, make his mind up on that.

"All the same... I would have still liked that larger piece. I don't suppose there is any chance of another?"

Almost by way of an answer, another wave thundered ashore. Bigger even than the one which had snatched the previous deep orange gift away.

Was that a coincidence or nature's way of replying? Who could say? Either way, it was clearly time to move a little further back from the sea, to examine more closely his finds of the day, and perhaps light a small fire, and cook a few fish. As freshly caught as the amber was found.

There were several places, along the Baltic coast, where Frode regularly visited to collect amber. Usually deposited after a storm, the stuff could sometimes be found in abundance. Of course people who lived nearby would also collect the amber, but there were one or two places, in particular, which they avoided due to local superstitions. Places considered evil, dark or unholy.

And Frode was at one of those places today.

A long, almost claw like extension of land, which reached a couple of miles out into the sea. The terrain was flat, festooned with low sand dunes and covered with a coarse, salty, grass. It could be dismal in rain or under a heavy grey sky. And at such times, truly, Frode felt that evil too. Felt it or imagined it? It was impossible to say which.

Though it was much harder to feel such things on a day like this one, a day where the sun shone and the birds called from overhead or from within their nests out on the spartan grasses.

And as Frode half sat, half lay, on one of the innumerable low sand dunes, with a small fire now baking his dinner, a large leather pouch partially filled with amber, he felt that there were few better places to be.

"Evil spirits", he said. "Maybe they like a bit of space. Some quiet. To get away from people. And when there's no-one around, perhaps they stop being evil and just sit back like this and enjoy the sun".

He laughed at that idea.

Then he sat upright. Stood. Stopped laughing. And suddenly he felt a lot more uneasy.

There, in the middle distance, silhouetted against the pale blue sky, was the unmistakable shape of a man, a man leading a horse. And heading very much in this isolated and remote direction.

The claw shaped spit of land had no established tracks upon it. Locals avoided it, and rare visitors such as Frode were too infrequent to make or leave a proper path.

So why would a man be leading a horse out here? Nobody would use a horse to collect amber. And there was surely no other reason for coming out onto this inhospitable scrap of land.

Frode checked his belongings, scattered carelessly around him on the sand.

He had weapons. Of course he did. This was the Iron Age, nobody went anywhere without several blades of one kind or another. And so he squatted down, picked up a dagger, and tucked it into the top of his boot. Then he picked up a second knife and tucked that one into his belt.

Then, and carefully, he moved away from the fire.

The smell and smoke of which would be a sure giveaway to the rapidly approaching traveller. Too late to bother to put the fire out. Whoever it was would already have the scent of it.

Frode moved away, behind another low sand dune, and lay flat on his stomach, peering through some coarse grass. Watching as the man leading the horse came ever closer.

Closer.

Closer.

And closer.

2

"Tormod! Is that really you?"

Frode stood. No more need to be hidden. This was a friend, a very out of place friend, but a friend of many years standing nonetheless.

"And is that truly Kvid you still ride?"

The man, Tormod, let go of the rope, by which he had led the horse, through the uneasy landscape. In all probability, the horse had no need of being led, it would have followed Tormod regardless. But the dunes, the shifting sands, the proximity of the sea were unfamiliar terrain to both man and horse, and each, in a way, had comforted the other during their long trek.

"Yes! It is I. And, yes, it is still Kvid".

The men walked towards one another, and took hold of wrists by way of greeting.

Tormod was tall, strongly-built and, at about forty years of age, almost a full decade older than Frode. He had virtually black hair, and a thick dark beard to match.

"And is it really you, Frode?"

Frode smiled. A broad and warm smile. "Yes. I am me. Or at least I was the last time I looked! And you, as ever, have arrived just in time to share some food with me. Fresh fish caught and just now, freshly cooked".

Tormod nodded. "Ah! Now that much I knew for definite quite some distance back. The wind from the coast carried the smell well in land. And, to be honest, had you been some stranger, some ne'er do well, I would still have insisted on stopping by to share your meal, so good does it smell!"

Frode laughed. They both did.

And together, the two of them... the three of them, Kvid included, walked easily towards the fire.

The fish was ready to eat, more than ready to eat, and both men had chunks of rather dry, coarse but still edible bread. And that, with the fresh air, the slightly overdone fish, the sound of the waves and small flask of ale each, made for a fine supper at the end of a long day.

They ate the food in silence, more or less, not talking but instead allowing their minds to clear and their bodies to digest.

Silence, whilst eating, unless at a special feast or celebration, was the norm in those days, a sign of respect for one another, for the food and most of all for the gods or whatever it was that was responsible for delivering the food on any particular occasion.

Then, with the light starting to fade, and although it would still be some hours until sunset proper, they both settled back into the soft sand of the dunes, watching for a while the clear and clean empty skies overhead and listening to the evening calls of the birds which so loved this strangely barren landscape. And only the sound of Kvid, seemingly happy to feed on the coarse grass, tugging at it, munching on it, seemed slightly out of place.

"You know, I believe Kvid is still the only truly white horse I have ever seen", said Frode, at last. "At least, the only one I have ever seen which was not meant for and soon put to a sacrifice. And wherever I see a white horse, it is always yours, always you, as sure a sign of your presence, as much a giveaway, as is your own face!"

Tormod laughed. "He and I are inseparable. Yes, that is true".

The fire crackled and spat as Frode tossed a few dried pieces of wood onto the thing and a few strands of salty sea grass also found their way into the flames.

"And did I ever tell you how I got him?"

Frode shook his head. "No, I don't believe you ever did".

"Well, he is what they call a fjord horse. Have you ever been to the very far west, the north west, where the land turns into harsh and barren mountains?"

Again Frode shook his head. "No. But I have heard it is always raining there. And in the winter, their wet snows often come early".

"Yes", said Tormod. "Yes, that is all true. It is not as soft as our land here, that's for sure. And I imagine that is why they breed such sturdy horses. Kvid, even after all these years, is as strong as an ox and good in all weather. He's not perhaps quite as sure footed in the forests as our own ponies, but for me, he is the best horse I have ever owned or am ever likely to own".

"And they are plentiful out there, such animals?" asked Frode. "In those hard and barren mountains".

Tormod shook his head. "No. Not exactly that. But Kvid, as you see, is a white horse, a mis-breed in fact, and they are very suspicious of such out there. But they do not sacrifice as much, or no longer as much, as we still do. That new god, he seems not to wish for it. So I exchanged him, Kvid, for a pony I was riding".

The fire dimmed a little and Tormod took his turn to throw a few sticks onto it.

"I always feel I had the best of the bargain".

It had been perhaps two years since Frode had last seen his friend Tormod. Both men were traders, and their paths crossed from time to time, depending on the seasons, the markets, levels of trade and other things. But where Frode collected and sold amber, Tormod dealt with horses or, more specifically, ponies. And where Frode's trade generally took him throughout the whole of what would one day become southern Sweden, Tormod would travel much further afield, even visiting, as he had just described, the distant mountains and fjords of Norway. (Though of course, it was not known as Norway at the time of this story).

It was good to see an old friend again. And both men were at ease in the company of the other. All the same, after talking for a while about their travels, and relating a few adventures, and after persuading Tormod – not without some difficulty – that the 'evil spirits in this evil place' would not mind them both resting there for one night, Frode could no longer resist asking the question which had sprung to his mind some hours beforehand, when he had first recognised the approaching man as Tormod; just what was he, Tormod, doing out here? To the locals this was a dank and haunted place. And there were neither wild ponies to gather, nor a living soul interested in buying horses.

"Have you decided to give them up, then?" Frode joked. "And begin to trade in amber?"

The sky above was now a deepening blue, and the small, low fire, gave the two men a more sombre appearance, more serious, as flickering shadows are wont to do.

"Ah, now", said Tormod. "Therein lies a tale... and my reason for this journey. A few days ago, I was in Ostmar. I don't visit it often, despite it being our largest town, because the people there, to my way of thinking, seem to have lost touch with real living. They don't know a good horse from a bad pig. But, on this occasion, I felt I should go because some large trading boats from distant lands had beached on the south shore with, or so I had been told, a view to buying some livestock. And not just any livestock, but cattle and, of course, ponies from which to breed".

"If this is going to be a long story", laughed Frode, "I promise I will not hear the end of it. My day has been long and I'm already sleepy!"

"No, no", said Tormod, taking a swig of his beer. "Not so long, be patient and try to stay awake, my old friend. I have made a long journey just to find you".

Frode sat up a little. "Truly?"

Tormod nodded.

"Then I promise I will listen, until the end of your tale".

"It is good", said Tormod. "Well... where was I... yes, traders. It felt like too good an opportunity to miss. The out landers had gone direct to Ostmar, as they knew it to be the largest market, the largest settlement. So I went there, too.

Even despite my growing dislike of the place. The crowds, the smells, the lack of space....".

"Tormod!"

Tormod laughed. "Well, anyway, you know of the sculptor there. You must know him? The little man who makes figurines, for sacrifices, for jewellery, all sorts".

"Per, you mean? The dwarf?" said Frode.

"Yes", said Tormod. "The same. A good little man. Quite brilliant really in his work".

"Yes, I know him", said Frode. "And yes, he is a good man. A friend almost. He has often bought amber from me and has created the most exquisite pieces. Hand carved. He is well renowned for his work, and justifiably so".

"Well, him", said Tormod. "He, Per, has been charged with murder, by all accounts".

"What?" said Frode, finding that hard to believe. "Per? Charged with murder? No, no. I can't believe that. He is a gentle soul. No. Never".

"Well, he has been so charged", said Tormod. "Gentle soul or not. And, I have to say, I am of the same opinion as you. I have met him once or twice, and yes, he is a good man. An honest man. Though, living in the big town, who can say how that affects a person, their character. It isn't natural to live like that".

"So... what has happened?" asked Frode. "What is the full story?"

Tormod shrugged. "I could not say, as I do not know all of the ins and outs of the thing. But I do know this much, Per has been charged with murder, and he has also ran away. Hidden himself somewhere. Which is doing very little to help prove his innocence, if innocent he is".

"It's serious then?" said Frode.

"Very", said Tormod. "And so, as you may imagine, they now have need of a verifier, at Ostmar. And, naturally, I thought of you in that respect".

The firelight abruptly faded, quite markedly so, as a piece of wood which had been burning brightly for ten minutes or even longer, suddenly gave up the fight.

"I heard you were nearby. Only a few days ride away. And I gave up my foreign traders in order to come and find you".

"Thankyou", said Frode, his tone, his expression, quite sincere. "And I mean that. Thankyou. You did well. I must go, yes. Per, as I said, I know him. Almost a friend, really. I must go".

*

Frode had to go. As a verifier, it was his duty. Though he would willingly have visited Ostmar, in any case, to do whatever he could for his friend, Per.

This was the late Iron Age, and society was beginning to take a rudimentary form, a shape and structure which would be recognisable right through until the late middle-ages and which even helped to shape our own world today.

But although there was a concept of justice, which varied from town to village, place to place, and which depended largely on the good will or otherwise of the most powerful members of the local community, there was, of course, no such thing as the police or, indeed, anything like that.

Over time, however, rather than allow an endless list of murders or thefts or whatever to go unpunished, or for the wrong people to be remorselessly accused, the notion of the verifier had arisen.

A person would be sent for, a verifier would be sent for, to 'investigate' a crime, in order to determine whether or not a murder had taken place, or whether or not the right person stood accused and so forth.

But there was no structure to this. There were no training courses, there was no uniform, it was not limited by age or gender. Instead, and connected with a deep reverence for the spiritual side of life, the position of verifier came to a person almost as a calling.

Such had happened to Frode. As a child.

A Grandparent had seen 'the gift' within him. A shaman had seen it too. And from then on, from an older man, another verifier, he had learned a lot about how to discover the truth, how to put two and two together, how to understand human nature. Trickery, careful thought, investigation, a knowledge of behaviour, help from the gods or spirits – if such there were – all of that, and more came into play.

And though Frode lived, from day to day, by trading the semi-precious commodity of amber, which would be turned into or used to embellish jewellery, he also worked, wherever requested, as a verifier. The Iron Age equivalent of a detective.

And just as with other chores in the Iron Age, it was a duty to carry this task out. Just as the smith had to work iron, the potter had to work clay, the herdsman tend to a flock, so too did a verifier have the duty to verify.

It wasn't a choice. It was a fact of life.

*

Frode set off for the town of Ostmar, early, very early, the following morning.

Tormod, having heard – or so he said – more screeches, cries and eerie calls in that one night, than he had heard before in his entire life, willingly accompanied Frode until the two of them were clear of the claw like expanse of land, and the 'evil' sand dunes were safely in the distance.

"You won't come with me?" Frode had asked him, as the two separated. "Do some more horse trading?"

Tormod shook his head. "No. No thankyou. One visit to the town was enough for me. If that is the future, everybody living on top of one another like that, then you can keep it!"

As the crow flew, it was approximately fifty kilometres or thirty-five miles from the beaches where Frode collected amber to the market town of Ostmar. Frode had no horse, and so, really, it was two days hard walk or three at a slightly more leisurely pace. This journey, however, he would split into two parts. On the first two days, he would walk most of the way to Ostmar, but then he would take the opportunity to stop, en route, and overnight, at the hut of a woman called Ebba. A woman who was, to the best of Frode's knowledge, the only other dwarf or little person in the whole of what would one day become the county of Scania.

In societal terms, Sweden, in the late Iron Age, was a true melting pot. The once reclusive natives, having had some limited contact with Rome in the previous centuries, now found their world opening up to all kinds of change as well as trade with their neighbours. And as a result of that, the population throughout Scandinavia, but particularly in the south and along the coasts, had increased markedly.

And nowhere could the 'modernisation' of lifestyles, the rising and falling of human tides, be seen more clearly than in the shifting manner in which people lived. And most starkly of all in their homes and houses which now came in a number of differing styles.

To begin with there were still 'classic' iron age dwellings of perhaps forty inhabitants or so. Fenced compounds consisting of a number of small longhouses or roundhouses and one large building. Clay walls, tall, steeply pitched thatched roofs and, in the large building, an open-plan living area and sleeping quarters with a fire set in the very middle. A simple hole in the roof to allow smoke to escape.

These were the homes of extended families, several generations all living and working on one site and they had been central to the southernmost landscape for centuries beforehand. Common to most of northern Europe.

Expansion from such basic dwellings came in the form of a man moving his family out from one compound and into another, usually constructed very nearby, where the 'new' family would then settle and grow, hopefully for decades to come.

But, by the time of this story, these extended family enclosures were rapidly disappearing, generally being replaced by villages or even small towns, though also sometimes by individual homes for people who wanted to – or had no choice but to – live out, outside of society.

In most respects, the villages were sprawling versions of those earlier settlements, but now, instead of one or two extended families living within a fenced compound, there could be dozens of such families and, in the case of a town such as Ostmar, a population running into the thousands. And that, that expansion, meant for a more structure community wherein defence and crafts and crops and hunting had to be thoroughly organised. And one ruler, one voice, usually had to be heard above the rest.

As for the latter... those isolated, outside-of-village houses, it very much depended. Some of these were built on good land and owned by people of wealth. These were places of power. Homes of earls, thanes and even, in some places, kings. But others isolated houses, individual homes, were at the opposite end of the scale. Many of these were quite temporary affairs, a small thatched hut, either round or rectangular in shape, often completed with whatever poor materials the occupant could lay his or her hand upon.

And it was to one of these wooden huts, alone, on a patch of very thin soil, that Frode finally came after a few good hours walking, towards the end of the second day of his journey.

Ebba, too poor to have any other name, was a little person just like Per. But whereas Per was already well into his mid-thirties, Ebba was only just over twenty years of age. She had no family, no kin, no children, nothing. And had it not been for a huge man, a 'giant' called Gan, also outcast from society, she would to all appearances have been completely alone in the world.

Together, Ebba with the almost mute Gan – who had obtained that name as it was virtually the only sound he could make – eked out an existence as an entertainer. The two of them would attend markets, special events, festivals and the like, often at an invite from a local lord or chieftain, and perform rough and tumble acts which people would generally find increasingly amusing the more they drank. Of course Ebba knew she was being laughed at whilst performing. She knew that people sniggered that her and Gan were an item. Which they were not. She knew also that people wondered what kind of a child such a union would produce. And more, much more besides. But she allowed it all to pass. Because the alternative, quite simply, in the harsh environment of Iron Age life, was to starve to death. Their land was poor, they, neither of them, could farm or produce goods to sell, and they had no money or other resources on which to fall back. Nothing. So Ebba, with the huge Gan, would 'entertain' for a living and ignore the barbed remarks and laughter.

"Gan!" shouted Frode.

The tall, muscular but obviously slow gentle giant turned. He was standing outside the front of Ebba's flimsy wooden hut, reaching up to the thatched roof – with ease – for some reason or another.

Gan grunted. Smiled. A broad smile. He recognised Frode and liked him because Frode was, it seemed, one of the few who treated both Ebba and Gan with respect. Treated them as fellow human beings and not as some sort of freaks.

"What are you doing, my friend?" asked Frode, looking from the big man to the roof and back.

Gan simply shook his head by way of reply.

Then a small soft voice spoke out. "We are repairing our roof. After the strong winds tore some of it out, only a few days ago". It was Ebba. Up on the roof. She stood, peered over the side, and waved at Frode. "If you give me a moment, I will be through here. And then we can all go inside".

Ebba packed a final bundle of straw into the roof, matted it out a little, then sat back to admire her handiwork. The job was done. And it was something to be proud of.

Gan then helped Ebba down off the roof, lifting her clear of the thing and lowering her gently to the ground.

The hut itself was made of aged wood, weathered grey, split in some places but repaired in others with a few new planks. Everything about the house said poverty. And yet, there was no question, that when Ebba showed Frode into the hut, it was evidently more than a hut, it was a home.

Furniture in most homes, at that time, was fairly basic. The richest may have had carved seats or even, in some cases, a carved wooden throne, of a sort. But the majority still sat on the ground, on loose bundles of straw or on rudimentary wooden benches or even, sometimes, on three legged wooden stools. And beyond such things, there was generally nothing or, at best, very little in terms of furnishing. Food was served in wooden bowls, or eaten directly by hand. There were no tables as such. There were few beds, at least not proper beds with bases and the like. And a home was, essentially, a place to simply sleep and shelter from the elements. In summer less so. But in winter, where working outside was impossible, due to bitingly cold temperatures and snowfall, then people would sit indoors all hours and work on handicrafts or even just sit and talk.

Nevertheless, the first thing Ebba did was to use a coarse, long-handled broom to sweep over some of the floor. Frode had seen brooms before, but only rarely. And it made him smile to see the young woman take such care of her home space.

"Sit, sit", said Ebba. "Please, sit. You will take some food with us, Frode?"

"Of course", said Frode. "Though only if you will, in exchange, share some ale with me?" At this point he produced a small flask of ale from his shoulder bag, "And, if I may, I would also like to rest here the night?"

"Oh yes", said Ebba, totally unflustered by the suggestion. "Yes, you can. Of course you can. You are most welcome".

She spoke a few words quietly to Gan and then the 'giant' disappeared outside.

"There isn't a lot of room in here, as you can see", said Ebba. "But Gan has gone to bring you a whole fresh tier of straw, to make a bed good enough for any".

Frode laughed. It was a kind thought. He could easily have slept on the beaten earth floor he was that tired, but he understood that Ebba wanted to show genuine hospitality. In all likelihood, given who Ebba and Gan were, visitors were probably rare, and overnight guests even rarer. That thought made Frode feel a little sad. But the sight of Gan returning, a few minutes later, with a gigantic bundle of straw put the smile back on his face.

"I am only small", said Ebba, "But I think you will find our food is plentiful. Because Gan has need of much of it. Enough for at least two if not more".

Fragments of food, cold meat, a pot of stew, dry bread, some goats milk and a morsel of cheese were produced and, without question, carefully and equally divided out so that Frode had as much as Gan and Ebba. The two of them then divided their own shares up, much as might be expected.

"Wait", said Frode. "I have a long strip of dried meat here, in my bag, let's have that too. I was going to save it for the rest of my journey tomorrow, but I would rather share it here, now, with friends".

"Thankyou", said Ebba. "That is most kind. I will not have need of it, but I am sure Gan will enjoy it".

The giant smiled, and made the sound once more from which he had been given his name.

Then the three of them sat, quietly, and ate.

Where most people walked by, without stopping, without even as much as a good morning, Frode had broken his journey to chat or to share a drink or a bite to eat many times at Ebba's house. But he had never spent more than a few hours there, never asked if he could rest for the night. So it was immediately obvious to Ebba that there was some other reason for this visit.

"So then", said Emma, once the food had been eaten, "to what *are* we owed the pleasure of this visit?"

3

"Ebba, I imagine you must visit Ostmar pretty often?"

Ebba nodded. "Yes, yes of course. It is our town, and not much more than a good walk from here. For you leastways".

"And you work there also, at times?"

"Yes. Quite often in fact. We entertain, the two of us, whenever there is a big market day or feast. A religious day. That sort of thing, you know. Anything like that. Not that we don't go to other places too. We do. We're usually very busy".

And that was true. Up to a point. At times of the year, the 'dwarf and the giant' were very busy, they were in demand. But at other times, weeks or months could pass without work and life would be hard, food in short supply. A lonely and difficult existence. Frode more or less knew all that, just as he knew Ebba was too proud to admit as much.

"Well that is good", he said. "I am glad to hear that. So then, would I be right to assume that you must also know Per, at Ostmar?"

Ebba glanced at Gan. Gan could understand every word, but could not reply, could not join in a conversation.

"Per? Oh, you mean the carver? The little man who makes all the figurines?"

"Yes", said Frode.

Ebba nodded. "Yes, yes, I do know him. He's a very gifted man but also... well, he's a horrible little pig. He hates me, because I perform for a living. He thinks we should be better than that. By 'we', I mean because he's a dwarf too, like me".

"I know", said Frode. "I have met him many times".

It felt strange to hear Ebba speak like that about Per. Frode had always found both Per and Ebba to be gentle folk, kind, and usually prepared to give others the benefit of the doubt. It was odd that Ebba should be so hostile. But, then, it was also something Frode could understand. If Per was opposed to how Ebba lived, felt that it was a slight on little people to entertain the way she did, then it made sense that they didn't get on.

"But have you heard any news of him, of Per, in these last few days?"

Ebba and Gan did not live on one of the four or five main tracks in and out of Ostmar. Tracks which were wide, well worn and frequented by travellers or traders of all kinds, and on a daily basis. Nevertheless, the quiet path they lived beside must still have carried news, relatively easily, as people passed by often enough for gossip of all kinds to spread. And given that it had taken Tormod a few days to find Frode, and another few days had passed since then, Frode felt sure that any news about Per must, by now, have reached the ears of Ebba.

"Per", said Ebba, shrugging her shoulders. "Per? Any news", she looked at Gan. "Have you heard anything about him?"

Gan vigorously shook his head.

"No", said Ebba. "No. I can't say that we have. Not really. But why? Why do you ask?"

"Oh, it's nothing. Not really", lied Frode. "I was on my way to Ostmar anyway and I just yesterday heard some rumours about him. Something to do with him having moved on, out of the town. Or something like that. And I was hoping to see him. For business, you know".

"Ah!" said Ebba. "Yes. He does live outside of the town itself, outside of the palisade, I mean. There is a group of small houses, outside, workshops, things like that, and Per lives in one of those. Perhaps it was that?"

"Oh, OK", said Frode. "Yes. That must be all it was. I thought I would ask you first, though, just in case he had moved on and you knew where he might be".

Ebba shook her head. "No. No, as far as I know, he is still there. Trying to live there like the rest of them".

The last time Frode had met Per, perhaps two years beforehand, Per had been living outside of the main town, in that same group of houses and workshops which Ebba had just mentioned. Indeed the first time he had met him, five or six years earlier, he had been living in that group of houses and workshops. And as far as Frode knew, Per had always lived like that, outside of Ostmar, below the great fence, ever since he had first arrived in the town from somewhere in the north.

Ebba stood, stretched and yawned. "Actually, it is funny that you mention it, Ostmar I mean, and whether we go there very much". She began wiping the wooden plates, bowls and things clean, using some fresh straw to do so. Stacking them tidily to one side as she did so. "There is going to be a special trading fair there next week. Apparently there are some important merchants in town, from across the sea, someplace or other, and the elders of the town have decided to provide entertainment for them. Gan and I will be going to that. Performing. Will you be in town for the fair?"

"In another week's time?" said Frode, "Yes. Yes, I think I could still be around by then. And if I am, then I will certainly look forward to it. Though I can never be sure, not really, from one day to the next where my travels might take me".

The following morning, a very basic breakfast was shared, and then Frode bid Ebba and Gan farewell before continuing on his journey.

An hour later and the path, which passed by Ebba's home, joined a wider track, which already had a few people on it, all heading in the direction of the town. And that wider track eventually merged with two or three others to become the

Iron Age equivalent of a main road until, finally, from a position on the brow of a low hill, the market town of Ostmar lay before Frode, like a smoky, brown smudge on the near horizon.

Towns, especially towns of this size, were new to Frode. New to the whole country, really. And whenever he found himself standing before one of them, the sight still came as a something of a surprise.

Even in the relatively dry climate of Sweden, where there would often be little or no rain for weeks on end, the main tracks to and through the town were often long brown smears of mud, in all but the hottest months of the year. Sometimes soggier, sometimes drier but still, and always, deeply rutted by cartwheels, footsteps, horses hooves, cattle, goats and who knew what else besides. During daylight hours, figures would continually busy themselves along those tracks, carrying large pots, bales of straw, a child, a dog, bundles of sticks or a heavy and salted side of beef. And everybody, everything, at this distance, appeared to be either one shade of brown or another. The array of thatched roofs, atop rectangular longhouses, sometimes still roundhouses, large buildings and small, were tan coloured. Fence posts, small and scruffy between patches of land, or the towering wooden palisade which surrounded the whole town, were other shades of brown. And from up here, atop the hill, even clothes, which in reality, up close, were made of many colours, red, purple, blues, yellows all appeared to be just brown. More or less. Everything did. It was all brown.

And above all that, above the churn of livestock, lives, hundreds of people, dogs, chickens, merchants, old folk and young, playing, working or talking, even at this mild time of year, there hung in the shallow valley, such as it was, a great pall of pale blue, sooty grey smoke. Because every single dwelling cooked over an open fire, and from every single opening, in every single roof, the smoke from those fires poured wildly up and out and into the blue sky. Lifted, blended together, twirled around, and then swept away by the days wind, which blew in, as it usually did, from the direction of the coast.

The smell of that smoke, wood smoke, blended with others, the scents of cooking, the smells of metal smithing, the burning of waste as well as some less pleasant but wholly natural aromas to carry on the breeze and announce the presence of the town for as much two or three kilometres in a downwind direction.

Ostmar. A brown world, topped with grey swirling mists.

And this, Frode felt sure, was the future: large towns, growing ever bigger. People living and working within them, coping with all the downsides of overcrowding and disease and crime, and being fed by a lucky few who remained in the countryside. It wasn't a world he had any great desire to witness. But it was probably inescapable all the same. As populations grew, it was an inevitability.

In this particular case, Ostmar, which now covered a site of some thirty hectares or more, had begun life as two separate villages. And it had only been within the last century or so that those two had merged, buildings and families, to become one large trading centre, which was now the largest single settlement in the whole of southern Sweden.

The town manufactured goods, such as equipment for horses, weapons and much more besides, and exchanged those for commodities such as precious metals and grain which were then exported throughout the rest of the land. As trade had grown, as demand for more skills had increased, so too had the population with many people abandoning small farmsteads which produced meagre quantities of food, to move into the town and learn a new skill or offer a service of some kind.

All of that meant that the two thousand or so people who now called Ostmar home, lived a pretty tightly-packed and crowded existence within its pointed, defensive palisade. And perhaps it was no surprise, despite the lack of external defences, that some folk chose to remain just outside of those spiked wooden walls and live a more insecure life, sometimes only temporarily settled, sometimes – as was the case with Per – happy to be attached to the town on a permanent basis, but still wanting an element of independence from it.

"Hallo! Hallo Frode! Stranger!" A voice called, and Frode peered into the milling crowd to find the speaker. Which wasn't at all easy to do.

Ostmar had three gates, one to the north, one to the west and the main one, which Frode was now approaching, to the south. Outside this gate was what could only be described as a squabble of huts and homes. And it was here, that Per both lived and worked.

"How long has it been since you last visited these parts?" Stepping out of the throng of people and animals, a thick-set man carrying three or four large pottery jugs, each attached to a very chunky belt.

"Alle!" said Frode. "I thought it was you, from the voice, but I wasn't sure. And I couldn't see you. It's so busy!"

Alle laughed. "Yes, yes. We are very busy here, as you can see. The crowds grow almost each day, at the moment, everybody from all over keen to trade. But it is not always quite so crazy".

Alle, somewhat appropriately given that his name almost matched his trade, had lived his whole life at the southern gate, offering a good drink of ale, from one of the pots he carried, to each newly arrived traveller. He made no charge for this but, in return for the service, the welcoming of visitors, he lived inside Ostmar itself and had an arrangement whereby his own food was produced by others and given to him.

It was a life he enjoyed, in part because he had his pick of the food without having to produce it or hunt for it, but also because it allowed him to stop and talk with everybody he met. Always asking about their news of the world outside, and always free with news of the town itself. And it suited his gregarious nature to live so.

"How long has it been?" said Alle, pouring a drink for Frode, into a small leather tankard, without being asked. "You must be here for the trade too, then? You've heard? a fleet of boats has arrived and they are very rich. Very. Looking to buy all sorts".

"Yes, yes, I heard", said Frode, accepting the drink. "But that's not what brings me here".

Alle frowned. "Ah! No? Then of course, you must be here as verifier. That business about Per, the dwarf?"

Frode nodded and took a drink from the tankard. There would be no need to prod Alle for any information, quite the opposite in fact, it would be hard to stop him from talking.

"A bad business", said Alle, shaking his head and lowering his voice a little as he spoke. "And who would ever have thought it? Myself, I am not so sure. They say Per attacked and killed a client. Of the death, well, there can be no doubt. But can you imagine Per doing such a thing? He always hated any kind of violence".

"Yes", said Frode. "It does seem odd. And yet I also hear he has run away?"

"Oh, aye", said Alle. "Which doesn't look so good for him, does it? The thing is, there was a witness, too. A reliable witness. One who swears that Per did it. And did it in cold blood".

"Truly?"

"Yes", said Alle. He looked around at the crowd of people, all busy, talking, trading, buying, selling. A few eating, some other drinking. Then, lowering his voice a little further, he continued, "his apprentice, no less. Suli, by name. A good lad. But go and see for yourself. Ah! But then you probably already planned to do just that, I imagine?"

"Yes. Yes, I will", said Frode. "And thankyou, Alle. And thankyou for the beer, too. It was just what I needed".

As a verifier, and even, often, simply as a trader, when visiting a place, however large or small, the correct thing to do was to go direct to the home of the chieftain or whoever was the ruling family. But Frode wanted to stop here first, in the tangle of scruffy buildings outside the main gate, to stop here and find out for himself, from Per's closest neighbours what exactly had happened.

The cluster of habitations, around the south gate, made for quite a warren of buildings and dens. Some of the buildings were small, just used for storing things or perhaps for one person to sleep in, whilst he (or sometimes she) decided whether or not to 'stick around' in Ostmar. Others, larger, were made of slightly more substantial wood and even, occasionally, had heavy timber frames. But they all looked more or less alike. And it took Frode a good few minutes to hit upon the little hut where Per, normally, would be busily at work.

Today, however, there was nothing. No sign of work. And the building even had a few pieces of wooden planking fixed across the open doorway. Presumably, Frode assumed, to discourage folk from entering. Probably put there by the elders of Ostmar, awaiting the requisite visit from a verifier. For whenever a death happened, which was unnatural, or somehow suspicious, a verifier would be sent for.

It was the way of things.

And this was done, not necessarily because the Iron Age had any advanced sense of justice which we might recognise today, but more, in a semi-religious sort of way because it mattered how a person died, and it mattered, really, because of the afterlife. So, in one way, the function of a verifier was also semi-religious. And Frode, and others like him, were a sort of cross between a detective and a priest. Finding out what happened in this world, to help ensure the right outcomes in the next.

"That is Per's place. The sculptor. But there has been a murder", said a thin and croaky voice. "So it is closed for now. Forbidden".

Frode turned to see an old woman, quite shrunken with age, seated in front of a tiny daub and dung covered hut, her fingers busily weaving an incredibly delicate basket.

"Yes, I thought this was his workshop". said Frode. "But I wasn't certain. Thankyou".

The old woman set the basket to one side and peered up at Frode.

"Are you here on business?" she asked. "If so, then you've wasted a trip".

"I am here on business, yes", said Frode. "But not for trade".

The old woman screwed up her wrinkled face ever more and peered at the stranger. "Are you the verifier then?"

Frode nodded.

"Ah, well, then *you* can enter! You can go straight in. Those boards are only to keep the curious out".

"I will", said Frode. "In a moment".

He stepped back a few paces to study the outside of Per's abandoned home. On either side of the building were what appeared to be sheds, used only for storage. And to the rear, he imagined, there would be some sort of latrine, for want of a better word.

The house directly opposite, though house was far too imposing a word for the structure, was the hut where the old woman worked and, presumably, lived.

"I hear Per had an apprentice who lived here too. Is he somewhere around? I am surprised he is not still here and working."

The old woman shook her head. "Suli, yes. A nice lad. But he is in the town. Staying with friends of the elders from what I gather. Don't ask me why, because I don't know. But, in any case, he's probably too afraid to spend time in there", she nodded towards Per's hut.

That was unfortunate. Because Frode would have liked to have spoken to the apprentice before anybody else. But if Suli was staying with friends of the elders, then there was absolutely no chance of him doing so. He would have no choice but to speak with the elders first.

"Do you know what happened in here?"

"A little", said the old woman with a very slight shrug. "Some man came in the middle of the night, went into Per's home and then Per killed him. A customer of Per's, they are now saying, but I'm not so sure. I don't know of any customer who would call in the dead of night, do you?"

"No. No I don't, not really", said Frode slowly. "I had no idea".

The old woman laughed.

In the middle of the night? Now that was strange.

"And what do the elders say?"

The old woman picked up her basket and began weaving it together once more. "Bah. You must ask them that. They are good men. Our town is well run. But what they say, what they think, it is their business, not mine"

"I will ask then", said Frode. "And thankyou".

He turned to look once more at the hut where Per lived and, usually, worked. The open doorway barred with only those few boards of wood. Insufficient to keep anyone out, but still a clear indication that one should not enter.

"But first, I suppose I might as well take a look in here".

Frode pulled one of the boards away. It came loose easily and fell to the floor. There was no need to remove any of the others, as he could step quite easily across them.

Inside the hut, the house, the home of Per and of his apprentice Suli, things were more or less as Frode could remember them.

There was nothing surprising about that.

Per was, Frode was certain of it, settled here, and more or less happy here, too. He was known, he was well respected and his work was widely renowned. So why should the interior be any different?

Thus, exactly as he recalled it, there were tools all over the place, some of which were incredibly intricate, and there was also plenty of evidence that Per was, as ever, busy. Not short of work.

Or, at least, he would have been busy if only this other matter had not happened.

But was it murder?

Was Per really guilty of murder?

In this little space? Within these wooden walls? And purportedly in front of at least one witness?

Frode stood, still and silent, trying to feel, trying to see, trying to imagine what must have happened in here.

But nothing came to him.

No clear or strong impressions.

The room, the hut, felt as it had always felt. Like a small home and a workshop, both things, combined. A tiny hive of industry.

Yet, clearly, something *had* happened. Of that there could be no mistake. Because there was a good deal of dried blood, more or less in the middle of the space. A pool of it, really, and more or less concentrated in one spot.

There was also in a thin sort of line leading away from that pool, a long but very definite line. And Frode recognised it. That line. He had seen it several times before: a man, stabbed, depending on where and how he is stabbed, may spurt blood. And that could form such a line, a trail almost of blood spots. Exactly like this. Though yes, it could also be worse than this, it could be everywhere. It all depended how exactly the man was cut and how soon he fell.

Frode knelt down. Examined both the pool and the trail.

The line had, in one place, reached up and onto the wall, almost at head height.

That also fitted with a stabbing. That sudden spurt of blood.

It was neither a pleasant sight, nor a pleasant thought.

Frode shook his head.

A fight then, clearly, and a stabbing, clearly, and yes, from that amount of blood loss, a death too. Of that, there could be almost no doubt.

But what else?

What else was here in the hut?

There was also a broken wooden board, which, on closer examination, appeared to have come from the side of Per's little 'bed'. And more than that, there were tools scattered on the floor, near that bed, and one or two partially carved objects too.

Frode frowned. Wasn't it always like this in Per's house? Rather untidy? Yes. Yes it was. It had always been like this.

But then... this seemed to be more than simply untidy.

Elsewhere? A low wooden stool was broken too. Something, or someone, heavy had fallen onto it, perhaps? Had the stabbed man fallen onto it? Before being stabbed, perhaps. Certainly not after, as it was not blood stained.

Frode then turned to the workbench. Festooned, as it was, as it always had been, with partially worked objects.

There were two or three large pieces of the highly polished stone known as jet. Jet was a very soft stone. Very easy to carve. But very difficult to add detail without breaking the thing. Yet Frode knew that Per could carve it. He had seen a necklace, once, which Per had made, into which a very decorative piece of jet had been set.

There were also a few small pieces of amber on the worktop. One or two more on the floor.

Some pieces of garnet. A deep red, semi-precious stone.

Some silver, too. Not much, but enough to be worth stealing if burglary had been the issue here.

And, finally, there was a good deal of bone, too – carved and otherwise. A material Per often worked with.

So no. Overall, it certainly didn't look as if Per had somehow interrupted a thief or burglar. Besides, who breaks into a place this size with somebody - in this case two people - living inside? That made no sense.

So had Per truly murdered a customer then, a man who had called here in the dead of night?

Frode stood stock still. Made no sound. No movement.

Looked into himself.

But no. Still he felt nothing. Absolutely nothing.

A verifier performed his or her duty using a number of skills or gifts: he would talk to people, find out what they knew, try to ascertain truth from lies. He would search for clues which affirmed or denied a story. And he would also use more ethereal means of discovering the truth of an event; he would try to feel his way forward, find something, some connection with the dead or the spirit world, to give him a lead.

Frode believed firmly in the first two approaches. And used them both.

He used the third approach too, and could not deny that it worked well at times. But, all the same, he often felt sceptical about it. Was there really such a thing as 'the spirit world'? Were there really 'gods' and so forth? He was not sure. Never sure.

All the same, he would usually, more often than not, 'feel' something where a murder had taken place. A killing. A death. A theft even. He would feel something. And yet here? No. There was nothing. This was a workshop where, judging by the evidence, a brief fight or skirmish had taken place and somebody had received a serious injury. But it had been no long or sustained battle. And there was nothing to suggest the need to kill somebody.

So perhaps Per was guilty after all? His apprentice said as much. And Ebba had called him a 'pig'.

"Perhaps I am wrong about him", said Frode quietly to himself. "Perhaps he had another side. A dark side. Dark enough to murder".

And perhaps that was also why he had fled?

Frode turned to leave the hut and then froze.

Down there, on the floor, right in the doorway, possibly even leading out into the lane, there was more blood. Spots of blood. No doubt about it.

He knelt down and examined it.

It, too, was dry, but quite clearly recent because little or next to no dirt had been trodden into it. And though the colour was faded, it was a few days fading and no more than that.

Was this more blood from the murdered man? Had he, perhaps, staggered out of the hut and collapsed in the lane outside? That was possible. But, given the loss of blood in the centre of the room, it was also unlikely.

Frode went back out into the lane.

Outside, and starting to weave a new basket, working on the base first and foremost, the old woman still sat.

"Did you see the dead man?" Frode asked her.

The old woman put her basket down. Sniffed, loudly. Scratched her grey hair. Frowned. "Before he died, you mean?"

"Yes", said Frode.

The woman shook her head. "No. Never".

"When he was dead then?"

Again the woman frowned. "You mean... before they took him away?"

"I mean, was he dead inside the hut, killed inside the hut. Or was he killed out here or perhaps died out here?"

"Oh no", said the woman. "Not out here. They had a fight in the hut, for sure, and he died in the hut, too. I watched them carry the body out. He never saw daylight or moon again".

And with that, she picked up her basket and began weaving it once more. Seemingly unperturbed by the recent events which had taken place in her neighbour's house.

Frode smiled to himself. He admired the woman's casual nature. Death and dying were no stranger to folk in the Iron Age. That much was certain.

4

The once, almost chaotic lay out of Ostmar had been revised several times over the previous half century or so. The net result of which was that the town now had something resembling a well-ordered street pattern and very few buildings which dated back more than those same fifty years.

Even within Frode's own lifetime, the last of the great Iron Age longhouses had still stood, more or less taking pride of place in the centre of the town. The sole remnant of the larger of the two villages which had given birth to Ostmar. But that building, too, had now gone. A wide 'street' which ran directly from the south gate to the north gate had taken its place.

The town still had the same overall feel, however. Of that there could be no mistake. A lively, strongly scented jumble of trades, animals and people. Far removed from the organised and almost tidy living of the Romans, who had built their own towns centuries beforehand.

Evidently the Iron Age had, in some respects, been a reversion to type for most of Northern Europe. And Roman ideals had been either forgotten or shoved to one side.

But once more that was all changing. Along with so much else. And something more akin to that Roman organisation was returning to places like Scandinavia, Germany and Britain. A movement of people which would slowly give birth to a more structured, in some respects more divided, in some respects more ordered society. One wherein clear rulers, and clear rules or laws, would come to play an ever greater part.

At the time of these stories, however, the concept of a single king and a single kingdom, as we know it today, was still more or less unheard of in Northern Europe and certainly in

Scandinavia. And in truth, the whole country which today we know as Sweden was still a collection of realms very much in flux and even, often, in complete turmoil.

And the reigns of any ruler were, usually, for very short periods.

Although there were kings, of a sort, and beneath them, there were earls and others, as to who precisely ruled what, and how they ruled it, justly or otherwise, was often a matter of dispute. And, often, of violent dispute. (Hence the short nature of so many reigns!)

Almost beneath the churn of kings and earls, however, and despite owing a loose sort of allegiance to them, were the rulers of individual areas, villages or, in the case of Ostmar, rulers of the town itself.

As this local position of power was often hereditary, these leaders, usually called chieftains, could be male or female. And although they, too, just like kings or earls, *could* be deposed, if their family squandered its wealth, or lost face through acting wrongly or if a more powerful, more warrior-like challenger arose – these local lords would often be from the same family for one or more generations.

And such was the case at Ostmar. More or less. Though, and almost uniquely, the town had two chieftains, or elders as they were known locally, with the head from each of the largest and most powerful families more or less completely sharing power.

Such power sharing was, really, a system doomed to fail. And during the Viking age, a hundred years later, Ostmar did endure a civil war of sorts. After which the town had only one chieftain. However... at the time of this story, the 'elders' and their families worked well together, and they were very widely respected.

"It is the verifier", a young man, carrying a drawn but at ease sword, introduced Frode into the 'new' longhouse with those few words, looked the visitor up and down once or twice, then turned brusquely on his heels, and walked out of the half-darkened building.

Frode had been waiting for almost a full hour to see the 'elders'. That was unusual, especially for a verifier, even more so in the case of a murder – but the young man, with the sword, had assured Frode that there was a serious dispute being heard, ahead of him, which concerned a large sum of money and which hearing was now reaching its culmination.

That hearing had finally, presumably, finished. A handful of men, wearing clothes unfamiliar to Frode which suggested merchants from overseas, had walked past him, and then a few men from Ostmar, presumably, had followed them out of the sombre hall.

Frode had tried to read in their expressions whether one 'side' or the other had been successful in the matter – whatever the matter was – but no, he could discern nothing in their faces.

Perhaps both had won.

Or both had lost.

Such was the nature of life.

The longhouse itself had been built very recently, albeit in the old style. A heavy timber framework, the walls made of clay and dung, the roof made of thatch. But now, unlike for countless previous centuries, nobody lived in the building and it was, instead, a status symbol. The central hall of Ostmar. A place where the council would meet, where the elders would make decisions on issues as varied as trade or justice, war or peace, fresh water supplies or extending the wooden perimeter walls. A town hall, almost. But a court house, too.

And as was often the case with these large buildings, when full, they felt convivial, alive with talk, firelight and song or music. But during the daytime, as now, hushed and either empty or in use for hearings, they felt cold, impersonal and darkly serious.

"You are Frode, the verifier?" said one of the almost statue-like figures who sat before Frode, in the dimly lit, smoky hall.

"I am. Yes", said Frode, taking a few steps forward, closer to the seated figures.

In front of Frode, three men, two old, very old, one younger, but still aged, sat on three high chairs. (Although chairs as we know them were still something of a rarity in the late Iron Age. These were roughly hewn trunks of wood, carved with a myriad of symbols of power and rank which served almost as thrones, rather than chairs).

The three men spoke quietly amongst themselves for a few moments.

Frode thought it odd, but understandable, that all of the elders were wearing thick leather breastplates and high boots, for all the world dressed as if prepared for a battle. It was, he supposed, also symbolic of power and position. The same was true of their gilded amulets, jewelled rings and so forth. Even their swords, which each wore, were elaborately scabbarded, jewels, figurative work. Symbols of power, yes. Of authority.

Doubtless, in their past, each of these men would also have fought their fair share of battles, both near, and quite possibly afar. But now, because of age but also because of family and prestige, they were the men who currently ruled Ostmar.

"Then you are here for the business of Per, the dwarf?" said the same man, again.

"Yes".

"He stands accused of murder".

The youngest of the three men then spoke. "It sorrows us to find Per may have done such a wrong. He was an independent character, lived and worked outside of our walls, he came from afar and was not one of our own, but he was a hardworking and skilled man and our town welcomes such people".

"I understand", said Frode.

The men spoke amongst themselves again. And then, the younger man, rose and came forward to Frode.

"We know of you", he said, stopping an arm's length from Frode before examining him from top to toe, much as the young warrior had done a short while beforehand. "You have a very good reputation".

"Thankyou", said Frode.

"Tell us, then, what do you know of this matter so far?"

"Very little".

The man slowly nodded his head. Understanding. "And what do you *feel* of this matter?"

The man was probably in his mid-fifties, and now that Frode could see him clearly, he saw that he truly was battle worn, with scars to prove it. But also, in his aged face, Frode saw wisdom, thought, kindness, consideration. This man was more than just a warrior who had somehow attained power. There was also an unmistakable nobility in that face.

"I feel...", Frode wasn't quite sure what he felt, but now was hardly the time or place to say so. "I feel that, perhaps, all is not quite as it seems in this matter. That is all I can say for now, in that respect".

The man took a step or two and stood directly in front of Frode. Almost challenging. Intimidating. But somehow, not quite at that level, not quite challenging, not quite intimidating. More... more... searching. Yes, that was it. Searching.

"Do you know why people kill?" said the man quietly.

The question surprised Frode. And, for a moment, he was not quite sure how to respond.

"Normally speaking, I mean".

"Well.. yes", said Frode. "Normally speaking. I think so".

"Then tell us". With those words the man returned to his seat, his place, with the two other elders. "And let us hear your views".

"Killing", said Frode, looking from one elder to the other as he spoke. "Killing, in my experience, people kill for one of four reasons. First, they kill for gain. Usually money, but sometimes for more substantial things like land or power, sometimes for something as little as a horse or a sword".

He paused.

"Go on", said one of the two older men.

"Secondly? People kill out of passion. Usually love, or hate. One or the other. In a temper, perhaps they kill a loved one, or maybe a rival in love. Someone who has won the object of their affection".

"Passion. Good and bad. Yes. And thirdly?"

"Thirdly? They have become crazy. Their mind has gone. Maybe they are sick or maybe a lust for power has gone to their head. It is hard to know which. And... fourthly... they kill out of self-defence, warranted or otherwise. This can be in a straightforward man to man fight, or one may kill another in order to prove himself to a crowd. That, too, is a form of self-defence. A warrior may do this, after a battle, where the person they kill has no defence".

The younger of the seated men spoke. "Are you justifying that sort of killing?"

"No. Not at all", said Frode. "It is always wrong to kill for love, for gain, for pride, to show prowess, those are all evil deaths. Outside of battle, it is only where one's actual life is in danger that it can be legitimately done. And even then, if it can be avoided, it should be avoided".

"Tell me more about the crazed mind", said one of the other elders. "The sickened head".

Frode shrugged. "I don't really know. It is hard to say. We know too little about the mind of another to say whether a person is truly crazy or not. We do not know what drove them to be how they are. For me, I feel, have always felt, that we have to make a decision based upon their actions and not on their intent".

"Crazy men are guilty of murder then?"

"Yes. Yes, I feel so. At least until we have some way of showing the workings of their mind, of proving they acted out of a madness beyond their control".

The three elders spoke amongst themselves for a few moments. Then, an agreement reached, the younger one spoke once more to Frode.

"So which, do you think, from the little you must so far know, is the case here, with Per?"

Frode frowned. That was a very good question. "Well, I have only just arrived in Ostmar. Only just begun to look into the matter".

"You have visited his house, though. Where the killing took place".

"Yes", said Frode. It occurred to him that news spread pretty quickly in Ostmar. "But still, I know too little to say. Certainly too little to be certain of what I say. I tried to feel my way, and could discover very little other than the obvious. A fight. Blood spilled. But I would doubt that Per was crazed, I have heard no suggestion of that. Nor is this likely to be a crime of passion of one kind or another".

"So a straightforward murder for gain, then?"

"No. Not necessarily, no".

"To keep the money his customer brought him and to keep the carved figurine which we must assume was subject to sale also?"

Again Frode shook his head. "No. To me, that seems very unlikely. Why would he do that now? Why this one customer? Why not many over the years? And besides, inside Per's workshop, I found plenty of evidence of wealth, albeit on a small scale. If Per killed for money, for gain, why would he flee and leave such things behind?"

"Perhaps he fled in sheer panic", said one of the other elders.

"Yes, that is possible", said Frode. "But there was also clear evidence of a struggle. A proper fight. If Per had simply killed a customer, would there also have been a fight? There may have been. But it seems unlikely".

"The dying man may have fought back, even whilst dying?"

"That is also possible", agreed Frode. "But I don't feel it is the most likely scenario. The blood loss in the hut... well, to me, that suggests the man would not have been able to fight back".

"Then what are we left with? Self-defence, you would seem to imply. Am I right?"

"That is certainly a very strong candidate, yes", said Frode. "It has to be considered, I think, in this case".

The three elders spoke amongst themselves for a few moments.

Then the younger of them spoke again to Frode. "Then why does Suli, his apprentice, tell us that there was no fight. That Per simply attacked and killed the man?"

Now *that* was an even better question. And Frode admitted he did not have an answer to it. Had Frode had the opportunity, he would have liked to see Suli before this interview. But, so far, he had yet to meet the apprentice.

The elders then conferred amongst themselves once more.

"We are in agreement", the youngest said, "That you may access any part of our town, our homes, as you see fit, in order to find the truth of the matter. It is important to us that trade and traders alike feel settled here. Per is, or was, a craftsman and one we were proud of. We have no desire to see him unduly punished, nor yet any desire to let a murderer go free, if such he is".

"I understand", said Frode. "And I can see how this is important for you, and for this town. It matters a great deal to you. I will respect that". He hesitated. "Can I ask what is known of the dead man? Was he from Ostmar? From somewhere nearby perhaps?"

"He was a trader", said the younger man.

"Ten days or so ago, traders landed at the coast. They came here. They are men from overseas. Brothers to us, but with very different ways". One of the older men spoke. "They are, to use your word, important to this town. They are buying a lot of produce and will return in future with more trade, if things go well".

"I understand", said Frode. "Was the trader with them? One of them?"

"In a way, yes", the older man continued. "Four men came with them, men who speak our own language, understand our own customs, to act as brokers between the outlanders and ourselves. The dead man was one of those four".

Frode nodded. There was nothing unusual in having such intermediaries in trade, especially where one party was from another country. He had seen it many times before where, despite the similarities of what would one day become Denmark and northern Germany, the linguistic and cultural differences could cause problems. And an intermediary smoothed over those problems. Helped facilitate trade.

"The four men were from hereabouts, then?"

The elder shook his head. "Their clothes, their words, differed a little. They are from the north, we understand.

Somewhere. But they have lived for some years in those other lands, across the sea".

"I see", said Frode. "I would like also to take a look at the dead man then, if that would be possible?"

The elders spoke to one another. Clearly in agreement.

"For us, yes, you have that liberty. We understand how a verifier works, that you may need to spend some time with the dead to see what you can learn from them. But unfortunately the dead man is no longer here. No longer with us. He is back with the merchants and they are at their boats, on the coast. Loading their goods. You will need to travel there to see the dead man".

Another of the elders spoke. "And please, can we ask a favour of you. Speak with the merchants from overseas first before going to see the dead man. Despite being from the north, talking our language, the man was nevertheless in their employ, not ours. Thus for good relations, for the sake of trade, we would prefer you to speak with them first".

"Of course, yes. I am more than happy to do that". said Frode. That much, at least, was not really a problem. But it was a nuisance that the dead man had already been moved to the coast. Though only a day's journey away, it would be time lost from the 'investigation' into the killing and sometimes, though not always, that could mean losing valuable evidence of one kind or another.

"I will set off for the coast as soon as possible, then", Frode added. "But could I see Suli, the apprentice, before I go? Would that be possible?"

"Yes. Of course", said the youngest of the three men. "In fact he should be here now. We had assumed you would wish to meet him". The man rose, clapped his hands and called a name. "Ulf, bring in the youngster".

The same young guard who had escorted Frode into the great hall, evidently named Ulf, came back into the dimly lit space, accompanied by a rather lean, worried looking, but handsome young blonde man.

The two of them walked across to stand beside Frode.

"Suli", said one of the elders. "Here is the verifier. You must tell him all that you know, and you must tell him the truth. Respond to all of his questions with the truth, and no harm will come to you. Do you understand?"

Suli, visibly somewhat awed by being in the presence of the leaders of Ostmar, simply nodded his head by way of reply.

"It is better to speak out", said Ulf gently. "Let your voice be heard".

The words were kind and well meant. And so Suli found the courage to speak up. "Yes", he said. "I understand. I will tell the truth".

Frode glanced at the young warrior, Ulf, and realised that there was, unquestionably, a family resemblance between him and the younger of the three men seated here. One day, it occurred to Frode, Ulf himself would probably be an 'elder'. Something that perhaps boded well for the future.

"Now you may question Suli as you wish", said one of the elders.

Normally, just as with any modern detective, Frode didn't choose to question people in front of others. He had found that to do so had a way, somehow, of limiting the responses and, possibly, even changing the very nature of those same responses. Because what people admitted to in private, and what they were prepared to say in public were often two very different things.

He also felt that it was better to be in a one to one situation because that allowed him to focus more on the individual, and carefully observe their body language. Again, in public, people often exhibited a very different body language to what they might show in private.

But this was one of those moments where such preferences would have to be set aside. And, after all, Suli was only a witness to events, not a suspect. So there was no reason for him to lie. Whether in private or in public.

Nevertheless, as the two of them spoke, Frode still tried hard to see, to feel almost, if what Suli was telling him was the truth, the whole truth.

"I understand you were present, a few nights ago, when something occurred in or around the home of Per, the sculptor?" Frode addressed that first question to Suli, and then watched the young man very carefully – though with subtlety – as he replied.

"Yes", said Suli. Not moving a muscle as he spoke, not turning to look at Frode, and standing more or less rigidly in front of the 'elders'.

Frode understood that posture. It could just be respect, nerves, both combined. This was, after all, Suli's home town. These men were *his* 'elders'. This was quite probably a very tense moment for the young man.

"It was seven nights ago", Suli added, helpfully.

"And what happened on that night, exactly? Seven nights ago."

This time Suli half-turned to face Frode, but immediately returned his gaze to the front. Facing the 'elders'. "It... it was just an ordinary evening. Per and I had eaten, we had both gone to bed. And then...".

Suli hesitated.

"And then?" prompted Frode.

"And then it happened", said Suli.

Frode looked at the elders. They were motionless, and almost expressionless. At this moment more like statues than real people.

"What happened, exactly?" said Frode.

Suli sighed. A large, heavy sigh. But still he did not move, did not look at Frode.

"I had fallen asleep", said Suli. "Then voices woke me up".

"Voices? Who's voices?"

"Per's. And another mans. A man I had not seen before".

"Where were they?"

"In the hut. In the workshop. Where I live. Where we live. The other man was near the doorway and Per was standing right in front of him".

"And what were they talking about?"

"They were angry. Both of them were angry. That much I was certain of. But they also, both of them, spoke in a strange language. Similar to ours. But different. I understood some of it, but not all of it".

"You were half-asleep?"

"Yes", said Suli. "But in any case, there were words I did not recognise".

"And what were they saying? I mean, from the words you did understand."

"Money", said Suli. "They were talking about money. Per wanted paying for something. And the other man did not agree to that".

At those words, and for the first time, Frode noticed that the young apprentice did shift his body weight. More than that, briefly, he seemed to look down at the floor, rather than directly at the elders.

"So what did you do?" said Frode. "Did you continue to lie down and try to sleep? Or did you get up and intervene?"

It was a question to which Suli did not reply. But Frode let it go anyway. "And what happened next?"

"Per got angry", said Suli. His voice suddenly quieter than before.

"Angrier, you mean?"

"Yes", said Suli. "I mean angrier".

"How angry?" said Frode. His own voice as calm as if he was asking somebody for directions or simply passing the time of day.

"Very".

Frode looked at the elders. One of them was now frowning.

"And what did he do?" said Frode. "Now that he was very angry".

Suli looked at the ground again. Then, with a visible effort, he lifted his face towards the elders. "Per stabbed the man. He killed him".

Frode drew in a long, slow, deep breath. Choosing to let the words of Suli hang, almost, in the darkened air of the great hall.

Suli, no doubt feeling the tension of the pause, shifted his weight back to his other foot again.

Frode watched the young man. A man who was now making a very deliberate attempt to keep his face fixed on the elders. A man who would not turn to face his questioner.

"So... you mean... Per had a weapon to hand. Already. And then he used it. He used it to kill the man. Is that what you are saying?"

"Yes", said Suli. "Exactly that".

Frode nodded. "And what happened to the man? Did he drop down immediately or fall through the open doorway back into the lane or perhaps stagger around?"

Per's home, like most homes at the time, had a doorway but no door. Not as such. In winter, mostly, doorways would be blocked up with a thick mattress of straw. Moved and replaced as the day began and ended. But in the milder times of the year, the doorway was often left empty, open, at best filled with a sheet of rough cloth.

"He... he fell... to the floor. In the hut".

"In the hut?"

"Yes".

"He did not go out into the lane?"

"No. He dropped down, slumped down, in the hut. Dead".

"And what did you do?"

"Me?", said Suli. "I... I was terrified. I thought Per had gone crazy. That he would perhaps kill me too".

"So you did... what, exactly?"

"Me? I... I got up. I put on my boots, and ran out of the house. I came into the town. I didn't know what else to do".

Frode looked at the young man's boots.

They were more or less the same as everyman wore. Calf-length, tied up with long laces, which criss-crossed the leg.

"Did you return to the house? The workshop."

"Yes", said Suli. His voice, the pace of his voice, quite definitely faster now. "With two men from the town, I came back. But the man, the stranger, was dead".

"And Per?"

"He had gone", said Suli. "He... he had run away".

5

Though still only in his early thirties, more or less, Frode had already met all sorts of people through his life as an amber trader, travelling between villages, isolated farms and towns. buying and selling, from old and young alike, during the harshest of winters or the longest of dry summer days. He had gained a huge breadth of experience, experience of people, of their lives, of the situations in which they found themselves. Some good, some wonderful, some bad, some awful. And that knowledge had served him well, had helped to serve him well, when working as a verifier.

Getting the best deal for a piece of amber could be like playing poker. It was a question of reading the other person. Seeing how far they would go. Understanding, or at least watching, learning and trying to understand, their body language.

Frode knew, mostly, but not infallibly, when someone was telling him the truth, and he knew too when someone was telling him a lie.

But he needed none of that experience, none of his acquired knowledge to see that Suli was lying.

It was obvious.

Frode had already been in the hut, where the killing took place. And it was small. Almost miniscule. And he had seen where Suli slept or, at least, where Frode imagined Suli must have slept – on a pile of straw almost in the middle of the floor. How had Per and another man met, and got into an argument, without already disturbing the sleeping Suli? That felt highly improbable. Suli, Frode felt, must have been awake, or at least woken, as soon as the man, the dead man, had arrived. Per would hardly have clambered, carefully and quietly, across the sleeping Suli in order to confront the man. To then attack him and kill him.

No. Suli had lied about that. Surely?

Likewise, the idea that Per had stood there with a knife in his hand, ready to kill their visitor, struck Frode as highly unlikely.

No more did Frode believe that Suli had fled in fear of his life, having ostensibly and almost calmly watched the killing without intervening.

But it was more than any of that which convinced Frode that Suli was lying. It had been the boys voice, his posture and even the words he had used. And it had been his refusal to look at Frode. To look him in the eyes.

But *why* was Suli lying? And to what extent? Had he, too, been involved in the killing somehow? Had the death been deliberate or had it been the result of a sudden and unexpected argument? And, on top of all that, why did the man call at the home of Per in the middle of the night?

Frode would have liked to have questioned Suli further. But now was not the time.

First he needed to go the coast, to see the dead man and to visit the traders from overseas. He needed to learn more about the background to this. To all of this.

And that meant setting off on a journey now, before any more daylight was lost.

"Ulf, my eldest son, will accompany you". It was the youngest of the elders who spoke. Who, in fact, turned out not to be an elder yet but was a heir presumptive, in effect.

(The way the system worked in Ostmar, was that two elders ruled, but a third would work closely with them all the time so that, in the event of a sudden or unexpected death, a successor would be ready to step straight in. It seemed an eminently sensible arrangement to Frode, where so often, elsewhere, there would be a power vacuum after the loss of a chieftain, and even, at times, battles would be fought to replace a lost leader).

"It is a kind offer, but there really is no need", said Frode. "I am quite used to travelling alone all across these lands. I have no need of protection and I am used to meeting traders of all kinds, even those from overseas".

"Yes. We are very much aware of that", said the 'heir', a wide smile forming on his bearded face. "In fact it is really for quite the opposite reason. You see, we wish Ulf to accompany you so that he may gain the experience. Not just for the travelling of which he has already done a great deal, but also for the chance to represent us, here at Ostmar. It will be good for him".

Frode nodded. It made sense. And he wondered again, though did not ask about it, whether Ulf too, one day, would be the 'third' elder, the heir presumptive.

And a short while later, the two men set out from the town to travel to the coast.

"If we make good time today", said Ulf, "We should reach the village of Satarp near to the sea in time for sleeping. Then we can go on to meet the traders, tomorrow morning, as that will only be a short trip".

That, too, made good sense to Frode. He had once spent a night in Satarp and, as far as he recalled, and perhaps because the little village was so close to the sea, food had been plentiful. Ale too. And the villagers seemed always ready to welcome visitors.

And so it was that, after an uneventful few hours of walking, the two men arrived at the small Iron Age village of Satarp. Where they were warmly welcomed, ate heartily, drank even more heartily, and slept well in piles of freshly drawn straw.

The next morning was fine. Dry, bright, sunny and once more quite mild. And they got underway after an equally robust breakfast.

It would take no more than an hour to complete their journey.

The town of Landskrona, in modern Sweden, was built on the site of one of the few natural ports in Scania. Although at the time of this story barely more than a small collection of basic huts stood on the site, the port itself was already a very important place because traders from overseas, who wished to visit Ostmar, the largest town for very many miles around, would all come ashore at this point.

Fringed mainly with reeds, the land around the port was incredibly low-lying and flat. And from some distance back, as they approached along the little river Sax, Frode could see an array of boats, beached on the flooding sands, and countless dozens of men working, carrying cargo back and forth, to the largest of the vessels.

Wooden jetties had been built out into the water, so that boats could moor alongside and loading could be done regardless of the tides – for here, unlike in the Baltic, there were once again tides, albeit very slight.

Some of the jetties were certainly wide enough for horses and carts, but some were much narrower, barely allowing two men to pass one another.

"If an army wished to invade", said Ulf, as the two men got closer to the boats, "This is where they would do best to land".

Frode agreed. And for all the world, it almost looked as if such an army *had* already landed. For there were four or five large cargo vessels, and a half dozen or so smaller boats, all of which appeared to belong to the same 'fleet'.

A few other boats, single, or in pairs, were further around the small bay, but these were clearly carrying out their own trading without any recourse to this larger group.

"We plan to build something here, as a result of that danger", continued Ulf. "A defensive position of some kind. But it's hard to conceive of the right approach, for we don't want to build anything which invites attack, nor anything which deters trade".

"Yes, I can imagine it must be difficult to find the right balance", said Frode.

A few more minutes' walk and the bleached reeds finally gave way to open sand, which in places was a treacherous wet mud, and beyond both sand and mud, the sea. Blue water which sparkled brightly under that morning's sun.

*

Centuries earlier, probably before Roman influence had reached Scandinavia, most boats in the Iron Age were no more than single logs, carved out to create rough – but still incredibly useful – canoes. These could be as short as two metres long or as much as six metres long.

Working solid wood to create such a boat, however, was time consuming. And although they served well for river and lake fishing, or for crossing such waterways, in the sea itself, such boats could too readily be lost. All that work for a very quick sinking.

The arrival of clinker built boats however, which by now were made even stronger with iron rivets, had made boat building more of a complicated craft. A number of men would now be involved in the production of a boat, specialising even, but the end result, of course, made for a much better vessel in terms of wear and tear. And whilst log canoes were still made and used by some, the majority of boats in the late Iron Age, when this story is set, were now manufactured in this more familiar (to our eyes) style.

The first of these clinker built boats were really no more than giant canoes, slightly resembling the later Viking longships, but smaller and lacking sails. And these, too, just like the log boats were still manufactured and used.

But in recent years – within Frode's lifetime even – sails had been added. And boats had grown in size too. Becoming slowly but surely ever more like the Viking longship.

Some of the 'new' style ships had shallow drafts, designed for speed. These were the sorts of boats which might be used by any invading army or, as appeared to be the case here, by merchants who wanted to travel and trade but keep themselves apart from their goods.

Others, of which there were at least five in the bay, as far as Frode could see, were even larger, wider and deeper. Great oak built vessels designed for cargo carrying and crewed by as many as thirty, forty or more men.

*

"It's like a small floating town", said Frode, as the two men approached the first of the ships. "I don't think I have ever seen so many boats, of such size, in one place before".

Ulf agreed. "It is the future, though", he said. "These men are from lands far away to the south. They have a lot of gold. And, in exchange, we have timber, iron ore, copper and other things. From here on, I think, we will be looking outwards more than ever".

The boats all flew the same black and white flag or standard. A black cross, on a white background, with an orange emblem of some kind in the very centre of the cross.

But the nearest of the ships was very clearly empty. A small, and shallow vessel, standing in water no more than half a metre deep, a narrow wooden walkway went out to the thing where ropes tied it in place. The almost flat calm of the water meaning that the craft barely moved.

The next boat, however, was quite different. Across the sands, which were fairly wet in this place, robust wooden boards had been lain extending beyond the jetties already in position. These boards allowed men to walk back and forth across them without getting wet, carrying an array of goods of one kind or another and loading the broad beams of the boat to what appeared an almost dangerous level.

The final boards themselves sloped upwards to the side of the boat, with the last few metres of planks directly above the water such that if anything or anyone fell, they would get rather wet.

"Hey, hello!" Ulf called out to one of the men, who was standing off the boards, in the sand, evidently taking a breather from loading items onto the ship.

The man looked up.

"We are from Ostmar" said Ulf. "We need to see one of your leaders. Are they on this ship?"

The man obviously didn't understand a single word and just shrugged. And for a few moments no one was sure quite what to do.

Then the man shouted to some of his colleagues who were already on board, one of whom briefly appeared, shouted a reply and then disappeared again from view.

All around work stopped. And men of all shapes and sizes stood and watched.

Then voices were heard and two different men appeared on the ship.

Frode could see immediately that one of them was dressed in an almost identical fashion to both himself and Ulf; a tall man, lean, probably about forty years of age. His hair was very pale, his eyes a cold clear blue. Whilst the other, who was shorter and darker, wore a long pale blue tunic of a style and pattern both of which were unfamiliar to Frode.

"You're from the town?" said the former.

"Yes", replied Ulf. "We need to speak to one of the merchants".

"Oh, well, then come aboard. Come aboard! You are in luck. This, here, is Blokk, he is one of the leaders of the traders".

"Does he speak our tongue though?" said Ulf, as men on the gangway made way for both him and Frode, to walk past and reach the boat.

"Not really. But I do. And I speak his language, too. My name is Vetle. I am from the north of these lands, one of your own kin, but for a long time now I have lived overseas and worked with Blokk and his people".

Ulf jumped down off the gangway and onto the heavily loaded wooden decks of the ship. Open, as they were, to the elements in much the same way as later Viking longships would be.

"You are buying up everything!" said Ulf. "I have never seen a boat so loaded. And you have many of them".

"Well, that is why we came", said Vetle, stepping aside to allow Frode to board.

"And it is very good, too", said Ulf. Then, half tuning to Frode, he added, "But let me introduce myself, I am Ulf, son of Bar-Ulf, elder presumptive at Ostmar. And this is Frode, a renowned verifier, he accompanies me or, rather, I accompany him, on this visit to see your late comrade".

Vetle nodded a greeting at Ulf, then turned to look at Frode.

Sometimes, when you meet a person for the first time, you have an immediate good-feeling about them.

Sometimes, it is the opposite. And that was how Frode felt about Vetle. There was just something about the man.

Vetle himself, however, seemed more than pleased to meet Frode. "Greetings, both, and welcome aboard!" said Vetle, smiling broadly and offering a wrist for Frode to clasp. (Handshakes *were* sometimes made, but when two adult males met, more often than not, they clasped wrists rather than hands).

Vetle then introduced the two men to the merchant, Blokk. Blokk smiled, also offered a greeting, and then spoke in a language not one word of which did either Ulf or Frode understand.

"He welcomes you aboard, thanks you warmly for all the kindness shown so far and bids us all to sit a while, to share a drink", said Vetle, translating Blokk's words into their own tongue. "And why not?", he continued. "It is a pleasant day, trade goes well, and we can take a few moments to relax whilst others work around us".

It struck Frode immediately that Vetle seemed hardly at all concerned about the loss of one of his men. Had things been the other way around, rather than make light of the situation,

Frode would have wanted a verifier to go and see his dead friend first and foremost. Certainly once initial introductions were made. But instead of that, and with polite and carefree words, Vetle offered Ulf and Frode places at a long wooden bench, which overlooked the lower deck, the lower deck where other men carefully stashed barrels and bundles of who-knew-what wrapped up in waxed cloth and leather. Blokk sat too. As did Vetle once. Then drinks were produced from a crock bottle, and poured into elaborately decorated horns the likes of which, as they took a good deal of time and skill to make – and had to be refilled after every drink – were usually reserved for very special occasions.

It all seemed very pleasant. Easy going. Convivial.

But at least as far as Frode was concerned it also appeared a little odd for what was, really, or what was normally, a rather solemn event; verifying the death of a person.

"You seem to be doing very well", said Ulf, good-naturedly, aiming the words at Vetle.

"I am", replied the Norseman. "Very".

Blokk toasted 'Trade between lands'. Vetle translated the sentiment. And Ulf returned the compliment.

Drinks were downed. And another round was poured.

"Wine?" said Frode. "And good wine, too".

"Ah yes", said Vetle. "I forget, hereabouts that is still something of a luxury or, at least, a rarity, is it not?"

"Very much so", agreed Ulf.

"Then trade will bring you much more of it", said Vetle, taking a large mouthful of the wine. Clearly used to having the stuff available and, quite probably, in abundance.

"So where exactly are you from?" asked Frode.

Vetle translated the words for Blokk, and the trader replied.

"We come all the way around those lands opposite, and quite a long way along the coast beforehand", said Vetle. "There we take a boat inland for some distance until you can see mountains, the likes of which I know of nowhere else".

"Do you refer to the land of the Gaul?" said Ulf. "I do not know of it directly, but I have heard tell of it. A land of sunshine, short winters, and plentiful in terms of foodstuffs. Wine too. But also great mountains".

Vetle shook his head. "No. The Gauls are, or they were, a little further west. But not so very far. Neighbours".

Frode shook his head. "No, I mean you. Where do *you* come from?"

"Oh", said Vetle, shrugging his shoulders, "A long way north of here. There are four... there were four of us. We made our way overseas many year ago. And it has been most profitable".

A man dropped a basket onto the lower deck and it split open as result. Spilling its contents in a heavily slumped sort of pile.

Brown, black and white, Frode recognised the flake-like substance immediately. This was copper, in a crude form, from central Sweden. People from Ostmar travelled north to buy the stuff, and now it was being sent further on these ships. The basket must have been hugely and horribly heavy.

Blokk seemed not at all perturbed by the accident. Vetle, however, was clearly angered by it.

"Be careful, you idiot. Pick it up and store all of that in another basket".

"They are good men, and they work hard", said Ulf.

"Yes. They are. But it pays to keep on top of them, all the same".

"They are your men?" asked Frode.

Vetle shook his head. "No. They are Blokk's men. They are his people. But I like to keep them working. That is, after all, how wealth is produced". Vetle hesitated. "For Blokk, I mean. For Blokk and for his people".

It struck Frode that those who did most of the work would probably see least of the wealth. That was a new thing, a new approach to life, at least as far Frode was aware, and it was an idea which seemed to be spreading. He didn't like it. To Frode, those who worked hardest should get the reward. But this was hardly the moment to say so.

"So then, if I may, your friend... your former colleague. I am sorry to hear of his death", said Frode.

Vetle helped himself to another large drink of wine. Then wiped his mouth with the back of his hand. "Yes. Thankyou. But you know, of course, that he was murdered. Killed in cold blood?"

"Yes", said Frode. "Or so I have heard. I am sorry for that, too...".

"Have you caught him yet?" said Vetle, addressing those words to Ulf. "He can't have got far, surely? A dwarf of all people".

"No", replied Ulf. "We are looking, but so far, regrettably, no, we have not been able to find him... Per".

Vetle shook his head. "It happens. Dwarfs. Anyone strange or deformed. They're all best off dead or at least put in cages".

Blokk, who of course understood none of what was being said, simply smiled and offered first Ulf and then Frode another drink.

Ulf accepted. But Frode, with a polite smile, refused. "I really need to go and see the dead man, now. If that would be possible?"

"Aye. Of course", said Vetle. "He was a good friend. A loyal soldier. We'd been together a long time. And it's important that the killer is brought to justice".

Ulf glanced at Frode and gave a small shrug.

"The furthest boat. The furthest cargo boat", said Vetle. "He's on there. We would, by now, have buried him at sea, in all likelihood, this place not being his true home. But the elders at Ostmar asked us to keep the body for you to see. To verify".

"Thankyou", said Frode. "It can help a lot at times like these to see the body".

Work on the walkway was suddenly interrupted as four more men, squeezing past the others, came aboard the ship, none of them carrying cargo.

One of these men, smiling, laughing almost, spoke directly to Blokk. Then one of the others did the same. And Blokk stood to greet all four men.

"These two are the other leaders. Of the traders, I mean", said Vetle, introducing the men to Frode and Ulf. "And these two here? These two are my own men. Auder and Ivar".

Once again, both Auder and Ivar were dressed in an almost identical fashion to the other Scandinavians. As the season was mild, they wore linen shirts, with coarse woven trousers. None wore any sort of a hat, though Frode was the only one of them to possess dark hair, the others were all blonde. Each man also wore a belt, as did both Frode and Ulf, and even, in the case of Ivar, a cross belt, with knives, purses and other odds and ends attached to the thing in a variety of different ways. Only Auder carried a short sword, also affixed to his belt. Trousers stopped more or less at the knee and, in the fashion of the later Vikings, all the Scandinavians wore leather boots tied up and kept in place with long laces, wound around the calves.

It wasn't that similarity in clothes which caught Frode's eye, however, but rather the fact that both Auder and Ivar had the same tall and very lean build as Vetle.

Similarly, that something, whatever it was, which Frode had not liked about Vetle, he now saw in these two men as well. And now, at last, he was able to identify it; these men, all three of them, had a darkness behind their clear blue eyes, a darkness which, at moments, shone forth. A coldness. A ruthlessness. They were warriors, yes, just like the elders in Ostmar. But unlike the elders, these men had perhaps lost any humanity which they may once have possessed.

Was it strange or wrong for Frode to so quickly assess these people? Perhaps. After all, he did not know Auder or Ivar at all. And he had only spent a short time in the company of Vetle.

But no. No. Frode lived by his wits, by his intuition. That was a big part of what made him a verifier. When something felt wrong, it usually was. And these three men *all* felt wrong.

6

The merchants, that is to say Blokk and his fellow countrymen, were friendly, smiling, welcoming even, and more than happy to talk. These were men who were clearly at ease with their business and even with life itself. And whilst Frode would ordinarily have been quite happy to chat with them for some time, to learn more about their homeland and their travels, now was not the ideal moment to do so. Conversation, where every sentence has to pass through an interpreter, both ways, is never easy. And where there is a definite feeling that you cannot really trust one or more of those interpreters... then that conversation becomes, at best, both stilted and awkward.

And after something which Ulf had said produced laughter, wholly unexpectedly, Frode had the distinct impression that not all words were being translated in quite the manner they may have been intended.

Indeed for a moment Frode even had the horrible thought that Blokk, and his many men and ships, really were there with the intent to invade or wage war. Just as he had briefly imagined when first seeing the ships from a distance.

But no. That was certainly a thought he could dismiss. There were absolutely no signs of weapons enough, or men enough, nor anything else, for such a purpose. Besides, ships were not loaded *before* an invasion, they were loaded with plunder afterwards.

Instead, and Frode felt sure of this, Vetle, as well as Auder and Ivar who also appeared to speak both languages, were simply using the linguistic confusion to amuse themselves. They were, and Frode knew it, that sort of people. Always looking for an edge, for a gain, and always ready to use others for their own ends.

"Well now", said Frode, standing, and addressing his words to Vetle, "I really must get onto my other business. Can you tell Blokk that it has been very good to meet him and his people? And tell him also that I wish them all the best in this venture, and in their future endeavours".

"Of course", said Vetle. "No problem". And with that he fired off a few quick sentences, not one word of which either Ulf or Frode understood.

"And he, in turn, thanks you for all of that", said Vetle, translating Blokk's words back to Frode. "And he wishes you well too".

One of the other traders then added something. Vetle listened, then translated.

"And they hope you will be present at the fair to celebrate trade, in Ostmar, in a few days' time. They plan to leave more or less straight after, before the autumn tides turn and the colder weather comes in".

Frode nodded. "Tell them thankyou. And yes, I hope to be there too. I am looking forward to it, in fact".

Once again Vetle translated. Blokk replied. And Vetle smiled.

"It is all good", said Vetle.

"I shall come with you", said Ulf, also standing and addressing those words to Frode.

More words, good manners, greetings, goodbyes, were laboriously exchanged, translated, exchanged again and then translated again until, finally, it really was time to leave the ship.

Walking off the boat, briefly, took Frode to a slightly higher viewpoint. The narrow gangway, still busy with men loading things on board, but a little quieter now, sloped gradually down, off the ship, and above the shallow water towards the permanent wooden jetty and, beyond that, to the sand. But here, just here, standing in the very prow of the vessel, Frode could see quite clearly into one or two of the other cargo boats as well. See into their low decks. Or, at least, he was able to get an idea as to what those ships were loading.

They were, all of them, it had to be said, much the same as this one. More or less full with barrels and sacks, and busy with people coming and going. Loading the last of the goods before their departure.

But it struck Frode that there was something missing.

"Vetle", said Frode, turning back to the small group of men who were mostly still seated and drinking. "Do these men,

Blokk and the others, do they buy livestock, also, from us? I mean, specifically, do they buy horses perhaps?"

Vetle frowned. "No. No, I don't think so".

He spoke to Blokk.

Blokk listened, then replied.

"Not particularly", said Vetle. "He tells me they would buy some, if good stock were being offered, yes. But mainly, no. They have no real need of livestock nor of horses. But why? Do you see any on the other boats?"

Frode shook his head. "No. No, I don't see any horse... I suppose... I don't know... I somehow supposed that they might be buying horses too".

Vetle shrugged. Shook his head. Then returned to his companions and his drinking.

The sounds of conversation and some laughter accompanied Frode and Ulf as they made their way down the wooden walkways and back onto sand and dry land.

"He seems not to be very perturbed by the loss of his comrade", said Ulf, as the two men set off to where the dead man lay on one of the other ships.

"No", said Frode. "I had noticed that too. It strikes me that he is not the sort of man to be concerned about such things".

"Do you know, I have travelled on one of these, the larger boats", said Ulf. "It was a few years back now, my father took me to where the Jutes live. Not there, directly across the water, but all the way around the islands, to the far side of their lands".

Frode nodded. The Jutes were the people who lived in what, today, is called Jutland, the main body of Denmark. But at the time of this story, they only lived in the most central part of Jutland with a few ports facing east, to Sweden, and more ports facing west, out into the wide seas and to places like Britain and the Netherlands. Britain itself, of course, had been slowly be settled by the Jutes as well as Angles and Saxons from other parts of Germany. But all of that had been some centuries beforehand.

"How was the journey?" asked Frode.

Ulf made a face. "The sea is not in my blood, I fear. And I have never felt so glad as to be finally back home. And on dry land".

"Yes, it can be rough, I know", said Frode. "I have also travelled through the islands opposite. And even once on a large cargo boat like some of these. I imagine it must be unpleasant if the sea disagrees with you".

The furthest cargo boat was also the least heavily loaded, the least full, and the least busy. And no more than five or six crew members stood around, seemingly unsure of what to do with themselves.

The cargo was all there, clearly, waiting to be loaded for their journey, but at present, much of it remained ashore.

Perhaps this was because the boat had a dead body on board.

Perhaps they were waiting for instructions to remove the body and load up with goods.

It was hard to be sure.

But sign language, smiles, gesticulations and the obvious difference in attire, helped Frode and Ulf gain ready access to the vessel and, eventually, to the point at where the dead man lay in the stern of the boat, under a makeshift tent of coarse woven material. And, once close enough, even without the assistance of a crew member to show the way, Frode knew exactly where the body lay. After all, a week had passed since the death, and early autumn whilst not summer, was still a mild time of year.

"Uck", said Ulf. "I've killed men. Two in total. And I will kill more when my town needs that of me. But I've never gone back to their bodies a week or so later to see how things were with either of them".

"I know", said Frode. "Yes, it can take some getting used to".

"Pungent. Do you need me to assist in any way?" said Ulf, clearly hoping that the answer would be no. Which, to his relief, it was.

Two crew members watched, out of curiosity, from a safeish sort of distance, and Ulf walked back to join them, whilst Frode examined the body.

Something which was, often, an unenviable task.

Lifting the material to one side, the first thing Frode noticed about the dead man, was that he, just like Vetle, Auder and Ivar, was blonde, tall, slim bordering on the gaunt, yet evidently well muscled in a wiry sort of way.

The clothes, too, were more or less identical to those of Vetle and the others.

So this was the right man. At least that much was certain.

But who was he? Who was he really? And how had he died? Had he truly been a client, buying something from Per, who Per had then simply robbed and murdered? That, at least, was the official story. But Frode, already, did not believe it.

Was already convinced that something else was afoot. But what?

A quick examination of the body did indeed reveal a major stab wound. Just below the heart.

The death, Frode felt sure, from such a wound would have been almost immediate. Which matched with the pool of blood, back in the hut.

The weapon used was also, quite evidently, more than a simple knife or the like. The puncture mark was too big for that and too broad. Clumsy almost. So no, this was a thicker object of some kind. Coarser than a blade, too. Suggesting that Per – assuming it had been Per who done the killing – had picked up the first thing which had come to hand, and stabbed the man with that.

But what *was* that weapon?

Frode looked closer.

It was hard to be sure, but perhaps an adze, or something like that had been used. The adze was a hammer like object with a sharpened edge. Short bladed, yes, but sharp and if, swung violently, with enough force, then dangerous enough to kill a man. It was the sort of tool that was used for rough shaping a large piece of wood, but which was equally often used for breaking tough ground, in much the same way a modern pick-axe might be used.

Force though... Force... Yes. That was interesting. Yes. It must have taken a lot of force to kill with such a tool. A big swing of the weapon would have been required. And so, logically, the killer must have been hugely enraged – or else incredibly desperate.

Frode wondered which.

And the blow would have required space too. This was not the kind of wound that could be inflicted at very close quarters, like a knife wound might be.

As for the rest of the man? What, if anything, could be learned from him?

Just like Vetle and the others, he looked hardened. As if used to living a tough sort of existence. Presumably he had also come down from the harsh north, and had also moved overseas some years beforehand to find a better life.

He certainly did not have the appearance of a man who would be easily killed. Nor, for that matter, did he look like a man who, in the middle of the night, would call in at a traders house to complete a purchase of some kind.

Some of his clothes suggested modest wealth. Fine patterns woven into his shirt, for instance. But there was no excess on show. No overt signs of wealth. And Frode felt that the dead man may have been almost reluctant to show how his 'new' life was making him wealthier.

This was a man who was proud of his roots. His toughness. His battle-hardened nature. He was making money, but still clung onto his past.

Next, Frode studied the man's lifeless face carefully.

No. This was certainly no trader. Of that there could be no mistake. This was a fighter. For certain. And there, right there, below his right ear, there was even a deep and old scar. One that could easily have been fatal but which, in this case, clearly had not been, for the man had lived many years after receiving that blow.

"How many battles have you fought?" said Frode to the dead man. "A warrior? Perhaps. Or a mercenary, I wonder? Did you travel where the pay was greatest? I wonder which, I wonder which".

A dull noise, the sound of footfall on the wooden deck of the boat, very close by.

Frode turned. Looking up and away from the dead man.

It was Vetle. Smiling.

"Did I say, that we would, by now, have buried him in all likelihood, probably at sea, this place not being his home and he's never going to see that again", said Vetle, glancing past Frode's shoulder at the corpse. "But the elders at Ostmar asked us to keep the body for you to see".

"Yes", said Frode. "You said". Not really sure what else to add. Nor was he quite sure why Vetle had left his friends behind to come to the boat to repeat himself. "It can be helpful to see a dead man, to try to discover things about him. It helps to find out why he died".

Vetle nodded. "Yeah. Yes, I imagine it can be".

Frode stood and allowed the sheet of material to fall back across the body, hiding it once more from daylight. And from sight. It was important, to Frode, to any verifier, to have peace, space and calm when examining a body. In part because that allowed a thorough search. And in part because, at times, something could be felt. A connexion. Something. Spiritual perhaps? Imagined perhaps? Who could be sure.

But Frode had just finished examining the dead man, at almost the exact moment Vetle arrived. So the interruption, on this occasion, was not important.

"And did it?" asked Vetle. "I mean, did it help to see the body?"

Frode nodded. Yes, it had, helped. But more than that Frode wasn't about to say.

"So now can we dispose of it? Him. I mean, bury him or whatever? We are all eager to be soon underway."

"Yes. I don't see why not".

As Frode walked away from the dead man, leaving Vetle issuing instructions to some crew members, it struck him how, generally, at least in times of peace, which this was, bodies were carefully and thoughtfully buried.

That was how it was done in the late Iron Age.

Burials, deaths, were done with ritual and thought and care.

Not this one, though. That was for sure. Vetle simply wanted to be rid of the body. The fact that he had, presumably, spent years together with the man appeared to count for nothing.

From the port where the boats were busy loading goods, to Ostmar, was no more than six hours walk. And the route was both busy and well worn.

Nevertheless, when Frode suggested that he and Ulf once again stop over at the village of Satarp, rather than go directly back to the town, Ulf offered no argument. Apart from anything else, it seemed to make sense to both men to stop and collect their thoughts, before reporting back to the elders in Ostmar.

Once again, as the evening drew in, the villagers of Satarp were more than hospitable, and food and drink were both plentiful. Long tales were then told about travels out to sea, and the strangest of traders who had been met.

But finally, as darkness set in and tired heads lay down to sleep throughout the village, Ulf and Frode had the time and space to talk.

"So", said Ulf, taking what seemed to be an age to arrange a mattress of straw to sleep on, "What do you think? And what will you be reporting to the elders tomorrow? There was something about those men, not the traders, but those others I mean, which I did not like."

Frode considered his reply as he watched Ulf try once more to arrange the straw in some sort of comfortable order.

Finally Ulf gave up with the mattress and just lay down on as it was. "Last night we had clean straw. This stuff has been used for cattle, I think. Are they trying to tell me something?"

Frode laughed. "Maybe they just don't get visitors this frequently and they've already used up all their good stuff ?"

Ulf laughed too. "Perhaps that is it. Next time, a week between visits, then". He yawned and stretched. "And tomorrow? As for that, what will you say?"

"Well, for a start, tomorrow, I will not be going back to Ostmar" said Frode. "Not directly, anyway. I think I have another visit to make first".

"Truly?" said Ulf, propping himself up one elbow. "Do you need me to come along, too?"

Frode shook his head. "No, no. No, it's just to see an old friend".

Ulf was clearly puzzled.

"It's alright", said Frode. "Friend or not, it is still in my capacity as verifier that I will be making that visit. My work has to come first".

"Ah, yes, that is good", said Ulf. "But I was asked to accompany you, so I should come along, really".

"No", said Frode. His tone adamant. "No. In order to learn the truth, there are times when a verifier must act alone. Quite alone. And this is one such time, I'm afraid".

Ulf nodded, slowly.

"Though I do thank you for the offer", said Frode.

Ulf sat up and tried one last time to arrange the straw, sighed, quickly gave up and lay back. "I shall return to Ostmar alone then, in the morning".

Apart from the sounds of a few folk sleeping nearby, for a moment, the inside of the rather small longhouse was quiet.

And Frode watched, as he often did, as the smoke rose gently from the fire, towards the hole in the thatched roof, from whence it would escape, twitching, into the night air.

"But what should I say?" said Ulf at last. His words hushed. The night still. But his tone also unsure. "What should I report?"

Frode took a long breath. Being a verifier was not about certainty. At least, not always. Things often turned on a hunch, a feeling, intuition. And, right now, that was all Frode had. And he could neither ask nor expect Ulf to report such things back to the Elders.

Nevertheless, something needed to be said to them. It was important. Very important. After all, Per was still being sought for murder, and at any moment he might found and brought to justice, perhaps even a summary justice.

"Tell them that I do not believe Per to have murdered the dead man", said Frode. "That, if found, Per must be held, he must be, but on no account should he be tried for murder".

Ulf had already sat up again. "Per did not kill him?"

Though lying down, Frode still shook his head. "I didn't say that. I am not sure of that. Perhaps he did, perhaps he didn't. But I am sure that he did not murder that man, as has been claimed. I do not believe that the dead man was a client, a client who called in the night, and whom Per then killed in cold blood before running away, perhaps, with a small amount of money or some such".

"Who then? Or, rather, why then? Why if Per killed... I mean, why run, if he killed for some other reason?"

"Self defence. Quite possibly".

Ulf nodded. "OK. Yes. For self defence then. I understand that. It can be so. And yes, let's say that for now. But why, if that was the case, did Per run away? And why did his apprentice, Suli, claim that Per did, quite simply, attack the man. Murder him in cold blood, as you say?"

"I don't know", said Frode. His reply honest if not exactly informative. "I don't have any answers yet. But that is why I plan to go and see a friend tomorrow. I think, and I hope, that I might find some of our answers there".

Ulf considered Frode's words for a while. "OK. Then I will do as you ask", he said. "I will request the elders to continue to try to find Per, but to simply hold him, until you return".

Frode, suddenly feeling quite tired, made no reply. His eyes were heavy and sleep was approaching.

"But you will be back in time for the feast? It begins on the day following the third night. This being the first".

"Yes", said Frode. "I will be back for that. Or at least I hope so, anyway".

The following morning saw a brief breakfast, a few bright farewells from some of the villagers and then Frode accompanied Ulf most of the way back to Ostmar before the two men went their separate ways.

Almost the whole of Sweden, not that it was called Sweden at that time, is covered in Forest. And it is a huge country. There are mountains in the far north and some open moorland too. And in the far south, today, in the modern county of Scania, there is a lot of open grassland and farmland. In between? The rest of Sweden is forest or lake.

Back at the time of this story, however, although Scania was already the most heavily populated part of the country and a good deal of land had been cleared for crops, woodland was still more than plentiful. And so within minutes of separating, Frode and Ulf were wholly lost to sight from one another. Tracks, Sherwood Forest style, disappearing into the trees.

And Frode had counted on that.

Expected it.

Because where he was going, the friend he was going to visit, actually lived much closer to Ostmar than he wished Ulf to know. And the best way to get to his friend's house, was really to continue along the same track as Ulf, most of the way to Ostmar. Which, again, was not something he wanted Ulf to be aware of.

But this was not a question of mistrusting the young warrior, but rather that Frode might have had to answer some awkward questions if Ulf had realised where he was going. And, so far, Frode didn't have the answers to those questions.

Moreover, who could say how this whole business would yet turn out? Frode certainly didn't want suspicion to fall onto his friend if they proved to be wholly uninvolved in the matter.

So for now, as Ulf went one way, all Frode had to do was wait a short while. He would resume the walk in the direction of Ostmar once Ulf had put some distance between the two of them.

And, after an hour or so, that was exactly what he did.

7

By now it was dark. Very dark. A blackness only ever met today in the most remote and rural of locations. Or else far out at sea.

But this was the late Iron Age. A time where night fall meant inky obscurity, more often than not. Where, outdoors, at night, a hand raised in front of the face would scarcely be visible unless the moon shone brightly.

Having made his way safely to the house of his friend, Frode had been lying now for a long time, hidden, waiting and watching.

Watching that same house for any signs of life.

For how long had he lain here, exactly? That was hard to say. Time was not accurately measured in those days. There were no watches, no clocks, no sundials. Nothing like that. A day was early, it was late or else it was somewhere in between the two. And the world was either light, or it was dark.

Very dark.

All around Frode, thin trees, with pale trunks, stretched up into the evening sky. Starlight overhead, but no moon. And in front of him, between where he lay and the track which ran past the house of his friend were bushes, scrubby bushes of one kind and another. Some of them would have borne berries, late in the summer. That season already passed. Others seemed only designed to catch or snag a person, neither of use as wood to work, nor even as kindling for a fire. But they did provide cover. And, on this night, that was all that mattered this night.

In fact, Frode knew well that those trees and bushes were only a bonus. For the key to remaining hidden in such a place, especially so close to a house, was to remain completely motionless and silent. Most of all silent. Because the slightest sound could disturb the chickens, geese, dog or whatever other animal or animals lived in and around the building.

It was odd how that worked. Yet work it did. Often the best way to hide from someone was almost in plain sight. Use a shadow, remain still, make no sound. People rarely suspected the obvious.

All the same... after so many 'hours' of lying here, and watching, and waiting, in an almost lifeless pose, it was reaching the point at which even Frode simply had to move.

And that, of course, risked setting off any one of those aforementioned animals which sounds, if made, would almost certainly alert the people inside that remote and isolated house. True, they might only suspect a fox or a lowland wolf, but they might equally suspect an intruder and come out to search. And they would assuredly do so armed. At night. In the dark. Searching. Armed. That could be dangerous. Accidents could happen.

So Frode resisted the increasingly desperate urge to move, to change position, to rest or flex tiring limbs. Resisted the urge to drink, to clear the parched tongue, to eat, to relieve the gnawing hunger pains.

But it was hard.

And as more time passed, it was becoming almost impossible.

Fortunately, at last, and quite suddenly, a small figure appeared in what could loosely be described as the garden opposite. A patch of poor earth, with a smattering of edible greens.

She walked a few paces away from the home to answer nature's call.

And with her arrival, a dog, their dog, started to shout.

"Hush up!" said the woman's voice, a soft voice, a kind voice, her words aimed at the dog. "It's only me".

The woman reached for the animal, tweaked it's ear in an affectionate manner and then, after a minute or so, turned to go back inside.

At this movement the dog barked again.

The woman laughed. Ignored it. And both returned into the house.

But Frode had already moved. Taken and used the opportunity. Changed position markedly. Stretched. Stood. And even backed some distance away from the house.

And now it was time for him to take a break. He would remain in close enough sight to see what, if anything, happened. But far enough back to be able to move. At least a little. At least until sleep took over.

And sleep did, finally, take over.

During the dark night which followed, Frode slept. Waking several times, in part due to the chill of the air, in part because he knew that he had to keep an eye on the house. His friend's house.

But finally, and without event, the night did pass.

Dawn arrived. Cool, damp and threatening rain. Frode watched the skies and hoped that it would remain dry. Not rain.

"Don't do that", he said. "Please don't do that".

The sun climbed higher, a slight wind arose, from the east, the driest direction, and soon the grey clouds were driven away and a pale sunshine broke through.

"Thankyou", said Frode quietly. His words aimed at the spirits of the weather, the world, at nature itself. Lying and waiting in the dry was one thing, and quite uncomfortable enough, but lying and waiting in the rain was another thing altogether. Miserable.

Frode glanced over at the small house, saw no signs of life, then moved around a little, realising once more just how hungry he was, he checked pouches on his belt for food and found that he had nothing.

There was, around where he hid, an assortment of mushrooms. But they were not good to eat. A few grub ruined boletus and, a little further away, a good sized patch of red and white amanita. There was no fruit in the trees. No berries left on the bushes.

He could now see the dog, the one which had barked the night before, roaming around in the 'garden' of the house.

Animals were usually much less inclined to bark, growl, shout, cluck, screech or otherwise give alarm during the day than they were during the hours of darkness.

All the same, a dog could still do that. It was far from unheard of. So, once more, Frode resigned himself to settle, stay, remain still, motionless and silent. To do nothing whatsoever as the day promised to be just as uneventful as the previous afternoon, evening and night had been.

And more time did pass.

Slowly.

Achingly.

So was he wrong, then? He wondered.

Mistaken?

Perhaps so. But his instinct said not.

Suddenly two figures appeared in the scrubby land opposite. One small woman, and one very tall man.

Frode, despite the hunger, thirst and despite feeling tired, made himself sit up and pay attention.

It was, of course, Ebba and Gan.

And the two of them, now outside, were practicing what could only be described as human juggling.

Gan, with ease, would lift little Ebba up, with a seemingly casual flick of his hand, such that she landed on his shoulder. Landed with grace, in fact. So much so that Frode, almost wanted to applaud.

Ebba then climbed up onto the giant's head. Where she stood. Stood on one foot. Stretching upwards. Pretending to peer into the distance.

Gan turned. Quickly.

And Ebba feigned to stumble and fall off.

But she timed her tumble perfectly, landing in the giant's outstretched hands.

From there she was lowered gently to the ground.

Evidently the two trusted one another implicitly, because such a performance could not be undertaken without such an understanding.

Then Gan disappeared. Perhaps indoors. Frode could not be sure. But he quickly returned with a handful of fire torches. He placed them on the ground. Lit, ablaze, Ebba them picked them up and threw them, one after another, in a pretend bad temper, at Gan. He caught each of them and juggled them. A circle of fire growing ever larger as his hands deftly turned the torches through the air.

And so it went on, for a short while.

Each taking turns to juggle, gambol, laugh, frown, shout and perform. Sometimes together, sometimes individually.

The fair, the fete, the celebration of trade, would begin in Ostmar the very next day. And, of course, Ebba and Gan were simply running through their 'act'. Making sure that it was all timed and done to perfection.

But fascinating as it was to watch, skilful and sometimes quite terrifying, this was not what Frode had come to see. And his aching muscles, and the lack of food and water, pulled his body towards sleep once more. Despite it already being late morning.

Ebba and Gan continued to rehearse.

Frode's eyes grew heavy.

And by the time he woke again, Ebba and Gan had disappeared.

"Dammit", said Frode. The words scarcely more than a whisper. The anger he felt, at himself, very real.

Frode had spent almost a full day, lying here, watching Ebba's house, to see if she would leave it, so that he could follow her. Instead, he had fallen asleep. And now some time, some hours had, clearly, passed.

Had he missed her?

Had she gone out?

Perhaps. Perhaps so. But if she had done so, then she was already back. Because Ebba appeared once more in her 'garden'.

And now there was something else.

Or, rather, someone else.

Something Frode had half-expected to see, but had not been certain of.

For coming along the track, not from the direction of Ostmar, but from the direction of the distant east coast, and appearing at first almost as a mirage, was a horse. A horse being led by a man.

A white horse.

"Kvid", said Frode to himself.

The horse, and the man, arrived. And Frode waited for Tormod to loosely tie Kvid to a wooden post, set a metre or so from Ebba's front doorway and evidently used for just such a purpose.

He then waited a little longer, for Tormod to be greeted by Ebba. Smiles, polite words. Two people who were obviously very good friends.

And finally he waited that little bit more for the two of them to enter the house. That poor, weather-worn hut in which Ebba took real pride. Her home. Her place in this world.

Then, and hugely relieved to finally be able to do so, Frode stood, stretched, and walked without any concern or fear of being seen or heard out of the scrubby woodland, which had been his own home for these last twenty-four hours or so, out, out and into the open.

Ebba's dog, which was lolling about the land, keeping a lazy eye on things, getting over-excited now and then by a chicken or even a wild bird landing and taking off again, spotted Frode immediately.

And it barked.

Not once, or twice, but several times.

And loudly too.

But these were not angry barks, these were not warnings, they were the friendly sounds of a dog greeting a familiar face.

And they brought Ebba to her front door before Frode had even had time to reach it.

At the sight of Frode, Ebba froze in that doorway.

And as for Frode, he stopped too. Stock still. In the very middle of the deserted track. Stopped and smiled.

"Well this is a pretty mess, isn't it?" he said.

Ebba, her face flushing red, smiled back. Whatever game she was playing, her and Tormod both, the secret was now out. Or was about to be out.

"Come in", she said. "Come in". And with those words, she glanced left and right along the empty highway, for all the world as if expecting to see somebody else out there. "I will explain".

Inside the little hut, Frode, Tormod and Ebba sat. Whilst Gan, following instructions from Ebba, stood outside, or at least sat and waited outside, keeping an eye out for any potential and unwanted visitors.

"I am sorry", said Ebba, for the umpteenth time. "I am so sorry. I had to lie to you, I had to tell you those things about Per. We had decided upon it. All of us. And it was for the best. We were trying to help Per".

Tormod agreed. "My friend", he said, the words warm and heartfelt, "And the same applies to me too. As soon as I saw you, out on those awful sands gathering amber, as we sat and shared food, I wanted to forget what had been agreed here, and I wanted to tell you the whole truth, inasmuch as we knew it. Still know it. But I could not go back on my word to Ebba, and through her to Per".

Frode shook his head. A lesser man, probably, possibly, would have been cross with his friends for their deceit. But Frode was no such man. He knew Ebba and he knew Tormod and he trusted that, without question, if they felt the need to mislead him, in order to help protect Per, then they surely had reason. Whether that reason was misplaced or otherwise. And it was not Frode's place to question them, certainly not his place to be upset or offended by what they had said or done when it was all, all of it, well-intentioned.

"It was, as Ebba says, done for the very best of reasons. To protect Per and to be sure to obtain your help in this matter".

"It does not matter, it really does not matter", said Frode. "When I hear what, exactly, is going on, I am certain I will understand it. And I would probably have done the same too, if a life depended on it. Though, to be sure, I would have helped here willingly in any case, not just out of duty, but also because Per is my friend too. But what, then, what did happen on that night? Tell me. I have to know."

Once more with a momentary fear of being found out, Ebba glanced at the front door to her home. She had no door, as such, only the space for one. In warm or mild weather, that space remained empty, unfilled, as was the norm in the Iron Age. And only in winter would a thick straw mattress, which served as a door, be placed in the opening.

Outside she could see Gan. He *was* seated. And not showing any sign of alarm. The track which ran past her home was quiet, then. Still and empty.

"He arrived in the dead of night", said Ebba, the words suddenly gushing out, though spoken quietly, gushing out as if she really needed to tell Frode, to tell someone else, someone new. "Per. He came to me from Ostmar. He had been stabbed, he was wounded, badly, and bleeding. And the journey here had taken a good deal of his remaining strength".

Frode nodded. He had already come to the conclusion, more or less, that Per had been wounded too. That the fight had never been just one way. The blood spots found in the doorway to Per's home suggested as much. Indeed, everything he knew about Per suggested as much: Per would not have simply attacked somebody. Of that, Frode was already convinced.

"He had been attacked, then?"

Ebba shrugged. "I cannot swear to that. But certainly he had been in a fight. Yes".

"He was bloodied and exhausted", said Tormod. "He stumbled into this place, and said little more than a few words. I was here, as chance would have it. I had stopped over. I was only passing by. Trading from west to east".

"You had not been into Ostmar at all", said Frode. The words not phrased as a question but rather as a statement of fact.

Tormod looked down at the floor. His lie, albeit a white lie, had also been found out. "No", he said. "I had not. I had heard of the traders, of course I had, and so I told you that story about my being in town".

"In fact they were not buying horses", said Frode. "But you weren't to know that".

"I didn't want you to think that we... that Ebba, Per and I, were all in this thing together, somehow. So I pretended to hear the news about Per in town. From strangers".

Frode smiled. "You hate towns. I found it odd that you would visit one. But I did believe you. At least until I saw the merchants and their cargos".

"I'm sorry", said Tormod.

Frode shook his head. "It does not matter, my friend. I understand". Then, turning to Ebba, he added, "And you, Ebba? I was convinced you had no liking for Per. That 'pig', you called him. You acted your part very well".

Ebba smiled. A small, almost timid smile. "I am", she said, "After all, a performer. It is how I live in this life. But I did not want you to suspect that I knew where Per was. I did not want you to think that he would have come to me. In case you told the elders". Ebba also looked down at the ground. Ashamed. "I am sorry", she continued. "I should have trusted you".

"I understand", said Frode. "It is alright. No harm has been done. And we can forget all that now. We must. Because what matters now is Per. What did he say when he collapsed into your home? How much did he say? And, as important as any of that, where is he now? Is he still alive and safe?"

"Yes", said Ebba. "Per is still alive. Just about. He is at the hut of the Crone, the medicine woman, a short ride from here. We carried him there, that is, Tormod and Gan carried him there, as soon as the dawn broke. He was very poorly from the loss of blood. But also, he was frightened, almost witless with fear. Though if anyone can bring him back to health, it is surely the Crone".

"Well that is good. That is very good. And I do know of her. The Crone. She is reputed to be a very good, maybe even a great healer. But what did he say? It may be hugely important."

Ebba frowned. "In truth he said very little that made any sense. Only that we were not to tell anyone where he was or even that he had been here".

Tormod nodded. "It is true. He spoke a little and then, more or less, he passed out. Only muttering a few words as we took him to the Crone. But nothing audible, nothing we could make sense of".

"He said nothing of what happened, I mean, of what happened at Ostmar?"

Ebba shook her head. "No. Nothing that I heard, no. Just that we were not to say his whereabouts. He was afraid. Scared. And very much so".

"I'm afraid that we're as much in the dark as you are", said Tormod. "The following day, we soon heard the accusations that were being made against Per. That he was a murderer. We did not believe that then, nor do we still".

Frode frowned. What to do? Or, at least, what to do first? Getting things in the right order. That was important. Could make all the difference.

"Let me serve some food, some drink", suggested Ebba. "You look tired".

"Thankyou", said Frode. "I am rather tired. And that would be most welcome".

Ebba gave a large piece of bread, soaked in a rich gravy, to Tormod and another piece to Frode. Pieces of fruit too. And some ale. She then took the same to Gan, who remained steadfastly on guard outside.

And, for a while, everyone sat and ate in silence.

Frode taking the opportunity to think. Think clearly. What to do? Should he go and see Per first? Or should he go to Ostmar?

The food and drink were soon finished.

"As I understand it", said Frode, passing his empty plate and beaker to Ebba who took them and cleaned them scrupulously, just as she had done before, "it is the word of Suli, the apprentice, which weighs most heavily against Per. I shall return to Ostmar first thing in the morning, and speak with the boy again".

Gan came back into the hut, motioned to Ebba that some folk were about to pass the cottage. And, whilst they did so, all talk about Per and Suli was dropped.

Ebba went out to speak with the travellers. Exchanging a few polite words, a joke or two. And after passing some news of the world back and forth, they soon resumed their journey.

"Just two poor folk like myself", she said, coming back into the house. "I have known mice with more wits. We have nothing to fear from either of them".

"You and Gan will attend the fair tomorrow?" Frode asked her.

"Yes. We plan to go in the afternoon and remain there until the following day. There will be a big fire, tomorrow night, and music, singing".

Frode nodded. "Good. That is good. And Per? I need to see him, too. But, if you can promise me he is well cared for and safe, then that can wait until after I have spoken at Ostmar".

"He is safe. And I believe he is healing", said Ebba.

"And will you be going to see him before the fete?"

Ebba glanced up at the doorway, Gan once more sitting outside in the lane. Hesitating, briefly, considering her reply. "Yes. Yes, I think I will go first thing in the morning. Then return here before going to the fete, together with Gan".

"I shan't be coming to that!" said Tormod.

Frode laughed. "No. I didn't think you would be".

"I like a festival, a fire, food as much as the next. But towns? No thankyou. If it's all the same, I shall rest here for a day or two and see how this business turns out".

"Yes", said Ebba. "Of course you can stay. You will, as always, be more than welcome".

Frode made an early start the following morning. Seeing the smoky, brown smudge of Ostmar, from atop the low hill, before most of its occupants had even finished their breakfasts.

He stopped, first, and briefly, outside the great wooden palisade, which defended the town, to re-visit Per's hut, home and workshop.

It took him less than three minutes to find an adze, the very tool – in this case the very weapon, with signs of blood on the blade – which had inflicted the fatal blow on the late night visitor to the hut. It had been discarded and covered half-heartedly with straw. Perhaps that covering had been accidental, when the hut was searched, as it must have been, after the killing. Or perhaps it had been concealed deliberately. If that was the case, it had not been very well done. Hidden in panic, then. That seemed more than likely.

He also spent a few moments checking, or indeed verifying, an impression he had when first visiting the hut.

There was only one, small bed. Which must have been where Per slept.

Thus Suli, as tall as Frode if not slightly taller, slept where then? Where? There. Right there, in the middle of the floor. Yes. As Frode had thought it. He slept there covered, more or less, in straw. More if the night was cold, less so if the night was mild.

And it had been cold, last week, at night.

Not freezing, but cool enough.

With those two points settled in his mind, Frode had seen all he expected to see here. It was time to go and meet the elders again.

8

Despite the fact, or perhaps because of the fact, that Ostmar was holding an important fete to celebrate trade, Frode found himself ushered in front of the elders without any hesitation or preamble.

And, this time, only two men sat in the sombre darkness of the great longhouse. Sat on the carved wooden chairs or 'thrones', waiting to hear what Frode had to say. One of them was Bar-Ulf, the father of Ulf, and more or less understudy to the other elders.

There was nothing unusual in the lack of ceremony, however. After all, today was not a day for affairs of state, for trials or hearings of any kind, but a time for escapism, fire, song, good food, good company and entertainment. Festivals were hugely important in the Iron Age, and there were fixed celebrations every year. Around four or five in total. And on top of those there were things like funerals or gatherings for war councils, and so on. So whenever a 'special' fete was arranged – such as this one – everybody willingly became involved in the thing. It was a time to let go. To drop formality. A time to laugh, to live and to return, in a way, to a more primitive state of being.

But all of that, for Frode, and for these two elders, would have to wait for a while longer.

"You return in good time", said the senior figure. "You are, perhaps, a man who knows how to enjoy himself and would not choose to miss this day and night. But you are also a man, we hope and we believe, who has undertaken his duty first and foremost".

Frode bowed his head slightly. "I have done so. And yes, you are right, in this life, we all need to allow ourselves some good spirit. I try never to miss a festival. Least of all, an important one such as this".

The older man smiled. A warm smile. So warm that his craggy bearded face appeared, albeit briefly, rather like Father Christmas, before returning to its far more typical grave expression.

"My son Ulf has reported to us already", said Bar-Ulf. "And we must tell you that, so far, we have been unable to find the dwarf, Per. Had we done so, however, we would have held him, to await your news as you have requested us to do".

"Thankyou", said Frode. "That was wise".

For a moment nobody spoke.

Outside, clearly, there were sounds of men and women, boys and girls, not to mention the odd over-excited dog, already beginning to enjoy the day. Or, at least, the preparations for the day. And the thought crossed Frode's mind that Alle, the man who gave away free beer to visitors to the town, would be having a very busy time of it already.

"As for my news", Frode began, "I am, for myself, almost wholly convinced that Per did not kill the man, his visitor, in cold blood, nor for theft or anything of that kind, but rather in a fight. The causes of which, however, I have yet to establish".

The two councillors spoke amongst themselves for a moment or two. Then Bar-Ulf, the younger man, leaned forward slightly, fixing Frode with his gaze as he spoke; "That is good news. We like the man, Per. And to have charged him for murder would have been hard for all of us. But you remember, of course, that there is a witness to the killing, and it is a witness who says otherwise".

Frode nodded. "Yes. The apprentice, Suli. I am afraid, for reasons known only to that young man, that he has not told the whole truth in this matter. At least, not as of yet. Though I plan to go and see him, if permitted, as soon as I have spoken with you. Then, I hope, we will hear the full story".

Again the two elders spoke to one another. Voices quiet. Agreement soon reached.

Again it was Bar-Ulf who addressed himself to Frode. "If that is the case, and he has lied, then we will need to know why he has done so. We will also need to know who began that fight, and why. To kill in a fight, which one has not started, where there is danger to one's own life, to use a weapon defensively is, of course, no crime. Even where it results in the death of another".

A roar of laughter, from outside, broke incongruously into the dark longhouse, wholly out of place with the serious proceedings going on inside.

And for a moment, to allow that laughter to subside, once more, nobody spoke.

"I understand", said Frode, finally. "I will bring you all or as much of that news as I am able to discover".

Bar-Ulf nodded. Turned to face his companion. Spoke with him. And then the older man spoke to Frode. "Your conclusions are our conclusions", said the elder. "We will trust them as if we had made them ourselves. So now go with our will to speak to the apprentice. Return to us when you have more news".

Frode thanked the elders again, wished them a good festival, turned and left. Somehow, for some reason, and despite the fact that the elders were more than equitable men, he felt rather glad to be back outside, in the daylight, the pale sun, where scores of people were already assembling around a huge bonfire. The fire itself, of course, would not be lit until the evening. But long before then, the vast majority of the growing crowd, would already be the worse for wear. Or, put another way, relaxed and having a fine old time of it.

And Frode wanted to join them. Drink and food was now being passed around. Some were already dancing, in a fashion, and others were telling long and probably lewd stories. Old tales, repeated from one year to the next. And yet the day itself was still only young.

"Frode!" A familiar voice cut through the crowd. It was Alle, pushing his way past several outstretched hands to offer a beer to Frode. "How are you? Drink? Today will be a fun day, I think! A grand day."

The burly figure swayed a little as he spoke.

Frode laughed. Clearly Alle had already offered himself a good deal of the town's ale. "Hello, Alle. Yes, I think we are all in for a good headache tomorrow morning".

"Ah! But now then, you must first accept one of these...".

Frode shook his head and gently pushed the offered beer away and into the hand of a grateful passer-by. A young man who seemed almost surprised to receive the drink.

"I cannot yet drink, my friend", said Frode. "For now I am still on business".

Alle's smile dropped briefly.

Frode saw it. And gave the man a big hug. "Later, hopefully soon, very soon. We shall both drink a whole skin of beer together, this day. I promise".

Those words had the desired effect, and once more Alle's face was lit up with a broad smile. "Then I shall hold you to that!" he laughed. Disappearing into the throngs of people as abruptly as he had emerged from it.

*

In what was, in effect, a fairly isolated and rather remote corner of Ostmar, there stood a brightly painted house, rectangular in shape, with a thatched roof in good repair.

The house, one of the few in the town to be coated in a bright pigment, in this case a rather deep sky-blue, was situated more or less directly below the great wooden palisade. Sheltered by it. And not only was the property in good condition, but it was also thoroughly furnished – albeit in a basic fashion. Simple items such as plates, knives, and pots with preserved foods were evident, and all in good repair as if new. And for all the world, it seemed as if someone important lived in the house, someone important but, perhaps, withdrawn from the rest of society.

And such was in fact the case.

Because the blue house was actually the home of the main religious figure in the town: the priest or gudjan. Though titles such as medicine man and shaman could also have been applied, just as accurately. For none of them were exact, but each of them described, in part, what the functions were of a gudjan.

And though this particular house was on the small side of things, as with others of its kind which Frode had seen elsewhere, it was occupied by a tight knit group of people. Men and women, of all ages, who looked after the Gudjan. Some kept the house in good repair, others prepared food, others prepared medicines or tended the livestock which lived in the small enclosed garden attached to the house.

These were folk who worked selflessly, for the good of the whole community, and so it was, perhaps, quite natural that Suli had been placed here, with this group of people, partly in their care, partly to learn new skills, whilst the whole business with Per was being investigated.

"You are here to see Suli?" said a young woman, who greeted Frode at the door to the house. One of the few in the town to possess an actual and more or less fitted wooden door.

"Yes", said Frode. "I am here as verifier. And yes, it is Suli that I have need to speak with".

The young woman bowed slightly, and stood to one side. Allowing Frode to enter the home.

"I will bring him", she said. Disappearing from sight even before her words had finished their sounding.

Frode stood for a moment.

The room in which he waited was simple, basic and extraordinarily clean. Clean in a way that almost nowhere else was. Like the home of Ebba, it had been swept, but unlike the home of Ebba, it had been swept well, over and over, thoroughly, day after day. And anything, everything within the room, which may have been old or worn or out of place had been tidied away. Changed for items which were not worn or broken.

In later years, a few centuries later, the same building would probably have been called a church. Or perhaps even a surgery. But for now, it was simply the home of the Gudjan, shaman or priest of Ostmar.

Footsteps announced the arrival of the young woman again, only this time, she was not alone but accompanied by Suli. The young, blonde, tall, handsome apprentice to Per the sculptor.

"Will you need clear space?" said the woman, asking the question as if it was the most natural thing in the world. Which, of course, to her, as she lived and worked with the Gudjan, and understood the need for calm, for space, for privacy, it was.

"Please. Yes", replied Frode. "If we may have a little time to talk".

"Of course", said the woman. "I shall ensure you are not disturbed".

And with that, once more, she quickly and quietly left the room.

Twelve years or so, was all that separated Frode and Suli in terms of age. In terms of confidence, however, at this point in their lives, they could not have been further apart.

Frode had left his own home, in the far north, at a young age. Forced out for reasons of inheritance but also to pursue his calling as a verifier. Since which time he had travelled and traded all across what would one day become Southern Sweden, with no fixed home, living by his wits and through his ability to make real friends. Such a lifestyle, alone, required the development of a good deal of confidence – bitter failure and probably an early and lonely death was the only alternative.

Being a verifier, of course, Frode had built on his wandering, trading experiences. Countless times he had been obliged to meet the most senior figures in a farm or village. Countless times his life had been threatened or endangered. And, so far at least, he had come through it all more or less unscathed.

Frode was affable, calm, reflective, intelligent and above all perceptive. Sure of himself, in almost every situation.

Suli, by contrast, given his own particularly hard start in life, was almost retarded by comparison. Younger, in most respects, than his years. Scared of the world, and out of his comfort zone as soon as he was outside of Per's little hut.

Frode could see most of that, in a glance, when he studied the young man. It was there in Suli's body language, in his posture, and when he spoke, it was there in his quiet manner.

But for all that, and from everything that Frode had heard of the boy, Suli was a good lad. Hard working and willing to learn. Respectful of his elders and of no trouble to anyone.

Or, at least, he had been no trouble to anyone, until now.

The question was, how best to approach the shy boy, in order to get him to open up and tell the truth...

"Suli", began Frode, "it is good to see you again. I have journeyed a lot since last we met. And I have much to tell you. But first, may I ask, how you are and whether you are comfortable here? These are good people, are they not? I imagine they look after you very well."

Suli, also standing, and unsure quite what Frode was going to ask him, or tell him, was quite visibly put out by Frode's seemingly casual and kind words. "Erm.. yes", he finally managed to reply. "I mean, yes these are good people. Upright and religious. They are... they have been kind to me. And I am grateful for it".

"And you? You are comfortable here, among them?"

"Erm... yes", said Suli. "Yes, I am".

Frode nodded. "That is good. That is very good". He turned away from Suli, and took a few steps across the small room. Then turned back to face the apprentice. Said nothing. And simply smiled.

Suli fidgeted uneasily. Tried to smile. But clearly found it hard to do. The situation was difficult. He was more than unsure of himself and of what he was supposed to do.

Frode allowed his own smile to fade.

Suli glanced left, then right. Then down at the floor.

Then back at Frode once more.

But still neither man spoke. And slowly, but surely, the silence in the room grew louder and louder and louder. So loud, in truth, that had it been audible, it would have become a quite deafening roar. So loud, in fact, that at last, Suli could stand it no more.

"So... then... is there something you want... I mean, if not, can I go back to work? Perhaps?"

Frode shook his head. "Not yet, no. Not work. In a while maybe. That depends on you. But tell me first, Suli, in all honesty, what did you hear during these last few minutes. Here. In this very room. As we both stood in silence. This room. This place so full of spirituality. The home of the kind people. People who are looking after you. The home of the Gudjan. Your own priest here at Ostmar. What did you hear?"

"Hear?" Suli frowned. "Just now? In this room?" He looked down once more to the floor. The beaten earth floor. "Nothing", he said, at last, finally trying hard to look Frode in the face, but singularly failing to do so. "I don't understand. Nothing. I heard nothing. Why do you ask?"

"Did you not know that the Gudjan talks to souls in this house", said Frode quietly. "In fact he does that here. In this very room, where we are now standing".

That was true.

In the homes of priests, all across the region, Frode had been in such rooms before. And although they varied in size and furnishing, they were all more or less identical in the sense that they were spotlessly clean and, somewhat less mundane, possessed of an almost unearthly calm. And for the latter reason, if not the former, such rooms were easily recognisable.

"Did you not know it?"

"No, I did not know that", said Suli. "When he is here, when the Gudjan is here.... if he is in this room and occupied, I am not allowed in here. But very few people are. Oh... yes, so yes, I think you may be right, then. Perhaps this is a sacred space. I don't know".

"Yes", said Frode. "It is. Where we stand, right now, I have heard it said that all the souls of the dead can hear our every word in such rooms, and they can read our every thought". Frode smiled again. "Imagine that. The dead hear our every word. See into our own souls. Is that not quite an incredible thought?"

Suli shrugged.

"All the souls of the dead". Frode repeated the words. Saying each word, slowly, carefully and clearly.

Suli made no reply. None.

And then Frode quite suddenly changed his tone, from soft, kind, friendly, to hard and almost harsh. "What happened on the night of the killing in the house of the sculptor? Your friend and mentor, Per. And tell me the truth, this time. Here, in this space, where every dead soul hears your every word".

Suli's eyes widened. Hugely. His mouth opened. Ready to protest, to repeat the lies he had already told Frode. And he tried to speak. He really did try to say those same words again. But this time... nothing came out, no words, no lies.

He could not do it.

He could not make himself speak. Repeat the story.

"It's no good", said Frode calmly. "You can no longer lie, my friend. Not here. Not in this space. Your head may wish to do so, but your soul is now in touch with the dead. And it is far too afraid of what will happen to it, to allow you to lie again, in the presence of so many spirits. Here and now you must tell me the truth. And only the truth".

Once more Suli tried to speak. To tell his story. Those same lies.

But again the words would not come out.

What had happened? Today, we would describe him as having been hypnotised. Frode had learned many tricks over the years, as a verifier, lots and lots of ways to get people to open up, to tell the truth. And amongst those tricks, where a witness or suspect was obviously impressionable, as Suli clearly was, he had learned how to quickly and easily bring them to a state where they could only offer the truth. Where, as in this case, for fear of their eternal soul, they dared no longer lie.

"The truth", said Frode softly. Taking a few steps closer to Suli. "Tell me what happened".

As if suddenly wracked by a violent pain, the whole of Suli's body briefly shook.

Was that, too, a result of Frode's hypnotic words? Or was that, in fact, his soul determined to speak the truth at last and pushing aside all else that stood in the way? Who can say which. Whichever it was, the truth of what happened that night abruptly poured out of the young man...

"It was me", said Suli. His voice surprisingly calm despite the inner torment of his sudden confession. "I did it. I killed that man".

"I know that", said Frode gently. His voice reassuring. Calm. Once more kind. "Already engaged in a hand to hand fight, Per had no space to make the blow which killed the man, it had to be made with a big swing and from a few steps back. Somebody other than Per had to have made that blow. But why? Tell me why you did it. Why did you kill that man?"

Suli, straightening up, appeared suddenly older, as if the man inside was finally stepping out from the boy. "It was horrible", he said. "All of that day, Per had been short tempered, ill at ease with the world, but even afraid. Scared. I know him well enough to say that. To be sure of it".

"He was scared", said Frode. "Go on".

"Night fell. And Per went to bed with hardly a word. Which was also unusual for him. Ordinarily, in the evening, we are quite chatty with one another. The day's work done".

"I understand. Go on".

"I took myself to my bed", continued Suli.

"And the night was cold?"

"Yes", said Suli, eyes widening slightly as he looked at Frode. "Yes it was. How did you know?"

"You slept on the floor. In the middle of the room but slightly to one side. Under a very large pile of straw. You pulled that straw over yourself in part because of the cold, but also, I think, because you felt fed up. Per, as you say, had been short tempered all day".

"Yes. Yes", said Suli. "That was it exactly. I heaped straw onto myself and then fell asleep very quickly".

"Go on".

"And then... then... in the dead of night, I was awoken by a shout. Almost a cry. It was close by, very close".

"There was a man in the hut?"

"Yes", said Suli. "Yes. A man I did not recognise. And he had shouted and, as far as I could tell, he had then attacked Per. It was the cry of a man attacking".

"Per shouted too?"

"Afterwards? Yes, I think so. But with Per, that was more of a scream. Terror. Per was wounded, already. I awoke and I saw that. And the man was attacking him again".

"And then? What did you do? What precisely happened? Tell me."

"I stood up. I panicked. I was terrified. It was all so sudden. Like waking to a horrible nightmare".

"The man turned to face you?"

"Yes! Yes, he did. Before that I do not think he had realised I was there." agreed Suli.

"Because you were hidden underneath that great pile of straw".

"Yes. That was probably it".

"And what did you do?"

Suli frowned. Then, ever so slightly, he drew himself up an inch or so in height. "I grabbed the first thing that came to hand. I swung it. With all my force. I swung it at the man". Suli sighed. A big sigh. But his fear, somehow, had now left him. "It stuck. It stuck in him. A horrible wet feeling. Then I pulled on the thing... drew it out".

"An adze", said Frode. "It was an adze. I found it".

"Yes. An adze. I pulled on it. It came away. And the man dropped like a stone".

Frode said nothing. Allowing Suli to continue.

"And then there was silence", said the young man. "For a moment I stood there, uncertain. Then I remembered the wound. Per. Per was bleeding. Hurt".

"Go on", said Frode. "What happened next?"

Suli hesitated. As if trying hard to recollect the truth of that horrible night, to recover it from the lies he had been telling since. "Per... Per checked the man, the stranger. The one that I had struck. Per checked him, knelt down beside him. But he was dead. I had killed him. There was a big pool of blood. For a moment, I think, I must have looked as if I was going to pass out or something. I remember feeling weak and pale. Then Per told me to put the blame on him. He was adamant about that. Very adamant. He told me, made me. He said that I was to say that Per had killed the man. That, on no accounts, none, was I to say otherwise because my own life would depend on it. And his too".

"You tried to persuade Per to remain?"

"Yes", said Suli. "Yes. It was a fight. But it was a question of self-defence. Life or death. Per was innocent. As was I".

"And what did Per say to that?"

"He almost screamed at me. Just do it. He said. Over and over. Just do it. You must say that I did it, or else we will assuredly both be killed".

"And then?"

"I had to agree. I had no choice. I did not want to say that. But I had to".

"And then Per left?"

"Yes. But he was wounded. Dying I think. He ran off into the night. And I had no choice but to repeat the story he had sworn me to tell".

*

Suli, understandably, would have had no interest in going to see any part of the festival which was being held – which had already well and truly begun – in Ostmar. And Frode, naturally, did not even consider raising the subject with the young man.

At the house of the Gudjan, even when the priest himself was not present, as now, there would always be work to be done. And most, if not all, of the people who lived in and around the house, were not the sort to be overly interested in any kind of party.

So Frode bid Suli well, promising that he would tell the elders the full story and explain how and why Suli had lied to them. There would be, he felt sure, no come back on Suli. The young man had done what his master had asked of him, and he had done so in the most difficult of circumstances.

The question still remained, however, as to why, exactly, Per had made such a demand on Suli.

Why had he insisted, so forcefully, on being blamed for the death of the stranger? Suli himself had no answer to that. He had reluctantly done as Per had told him.

Likewise, why had Per not, as Suli had also asked, simply offered his account as one of self-defence? Suli, after all, would have vouched for such. And the matter, by now, would have been over with. Quite literally, dead and buried.

For those questions, to know the answer to those questions, Frode would have to wait until he met and spoke with Per. But that, as the little man was, according to Ebba, now on the mend, could wait until tomorrow.

Today, and most of all this evening, Frode wanted to meet up with a few friends, relax and enjoy the fete. After all, as to who killed the stranger and why, that much was now resolved. To discover that much, and to prove the innocence or guilt of Per, was why Frode had been summoned to Ostmar.

So, first off, Frode would report his news to the elders. His news regarding Suli. And then? Yes, then would be time to forget the cares of the world for a while, and eat, drink, be happy and perhaps drink a bit more. Just for good measure.

9

It was now very late in the afternoon, even becoming early evening. And the excited, happy crowds filled Ostmar's open spaces to such an extent that the town almost felt claustrophobic.

And as they drank, both Alle and Frode pretended that the size of the crowd was one more reason for sharing yet another flask of ale.

"So many people", said Alle, his words not yet slurring, but not so very far off. "And I've missed them all. Missed them. Most of 'e. I need another drink to console mysel'".

"You could never have kept up with them all!" laughed Frode. "For me, I've never seen so many folk in one place. It's crazy".

Two young women, who had already shared a drink or two with Alle and Frode, came back round for a drop more.

"Sit, sit. Sit!" said Alle. "I've almos' run out", which was not that far from the truth, because the festival had only been arranged a week or so beforehand and the scale of it, in truth, had gotten somewhat out of hand. So supplies were not what they could have been. "Ah! But not quite", he laughed, producing two as yet untouched, unopened stone bottles of beer.

The two women, together with Alle and Frode, sat for a while, sharing the beer, watching the world go by.

"If I'd collected a piece of silver off every man here", said Alle. "As they came in th' main gate".

"And woman", said one of the women. "Every woman".

"And child!" said the other.

Alle laughed. "Aye! Yes. All of 'em, all of them. Then I'd be a very, very rich man by now".

"And a very, very heavy one too!" laughed one of the women. "Weighed down with all that silver".

All around, in groups of varying sizes, people sat and talked, sat and drank, sat and laughed. The town itself would be providing food for this special occasion. But that was taking longer than expected to arrive because the sides of venison which had been retrieved from central stores were not cooking as they should. And so, increasingly, folk who lived in the town were producing supplies from their own homes to help feed the crowd. And Frode watched as one old woman, as thin as a stick, doled out ladles of a thick stew from a great iron pot which a huge young man carried for her. Then, from another house, and waving beer as he emerged, a man produced a great hunk of cold meat. Others, bread. Yet others, more iron pots filled with food of some kind or another.

It was becoming a truly communal festival.

And it was great to see.

"Did I ever tell you that story about the bear, that came into town one night...", began Alle, his full attention now on the two young women.

One of the women, feigning fear, widened her great blue eyes in surprise. "Nooo", she said. "A bear? Really? Here in town? Oh my goodness."

Frode laughed. He had heard the story more than once before and had no real desire to hear it again.

Looking around the crowd, and sitting perhaps no more than perhaps fifty metres or so from where Alle told his nonsensical tale, Frode noticed one of the elders. The man was quite unmistakable not least because of his size, and bearing, but also because he was still wearing the clothes of a warrior dressed for battle. Still the amulets, the jewellery and even the sword too. The one in the elaborate scabbard.

It was true that some folk, though not very many from what Frode could see, had indeed put on their finer clothes for the party. But most, by far, if anything, had done the opposite. With a good number, judging by stains, clearly wearing clothes for a drink fuelled occasion which they must have used for similar festivities in the past.

That thought made Frode laugh. And take another drink of ale for himself.

Then He looked back at the elder. Surrounded as he was, presumably, with family and close friends, he nevertheless sat out, here, in public, quite visibly laughing and relaxing with everybody else.

The thought occurred to Frode, as it had done before, that such a 'common touch' was a big part of the reason that Ostmar 'worked'. That connection the elders had and maintained with their own people.

It mattered.

Hugely.

Living in a crowded environment like this, it would be all too easy for those who ruled to become aloof, stand-offish and start to feather their own nests. But that was not how things were here.

And Frode wondered what would ever happen, in any such town, now or in the distant future, where once the elders, or the government did begin to act in such a self-serving manner. Forgetting about the people. Only looking after themselves and their rich friends.

Suddenly a gap in the crowds opened up.

Alle had finished his story about the bear, and the women were on their feet, as indeed were most people now, as a small procession of performers made its way into the centre of town to loud cheers, laughter and a good deal of applause.

At the head of the short line there was a man, or at least, it was probably a man, dressed from head to toe in an animal skin and mask. Growling, hissing and spitting, playfully, at the crowd as he made his way through them.

The smallest children in the crowd, pushed to the front by their parents, screamed and squealed as the 'animal' approached. Their faces full of joy and terror in equal measure.

The 'animal' passed by. Some of the bravest children following him, even tugging at his costume. Then he turned, and hissed and growled again, just enough for the little ones to run off screaming with delight.

Then came others, some women, boldly dressed in the most vivid of colours, who bore flaming torches. The light from which seemed brighter than expected.

It was already getting dark? Frode looked away from the procession for a moment. Up to the sky. Yes, it was darkening, quite markedly now. It would soon be time for the big fire. The performers would play in front of the thing, once it had been lit. And the crowds would draw in ever more around the fire. And the venison, or so Frode had just heard, was now finally being served.

Next in the procession came jugglers, men and women, tossing the most ill-sorted selection of objects as they walked. And doing so, it seemed to Frode, with ease. Their eyes more often than not, looking away from the things they juggled.

People saw that. Applauded louder. It was quite amazing that not a single object was dropped. Not one.

And then came Ebba. And Gan. Ebba dressed now in the slightest of costumes as, indeed, was Gan. And the hope struck Frode that, somewhere, they had warmer clothes to step into as the night wore on, once their own performance was done.

"Ebba!" he called.

The little woman came over to Frode. And the two hugged briefly.

"You look gorgeous", said Frode.

Ebba laughed. "Ah! That's because the better I look... the more we earn!"

Gan also spotted Frode, but being busy at the time lifting a tiny child high up in the air, to the squeals of delight of the infant, he had no time to come over to say hello.

And then, quite suddenly, both Ebba and Gan disappeared into the crowds. Crowds growing ever thicker as the procession moved towards the big fire, and people followed it in from the outskirts of town.

Another gap opened up, and more performers appeared.

This time it was a small group of musicians, mostly women, and generally wearing less clothing than was ideal for the time of year. This in itself brought a lot of extra cheers from the crowd, as did the semi-raucous nature of the music. A more or less cacophonous sound of flutes, horns, stringed instruments and even two large drums.

The racket – for such it was – was quite deliberate, however. The same musicians would later play softer and far more in tune, as sagas were recited around the dying flames of the fire, but when approaching a place of celebration, as a night began, just as when approaching a battle, the idea was simply to make as much noise as possible. To rouse the good gods or spirits, to bring them to the festival. And to scare away the ill.

And the musicians were certainly doing that. Rousing. And scaring. In equal measure.

After the musicians more figures appeared, but before Frode could make out who they were or what they brought to the party, the crowd swallowed him up, and took him almost inadvertently, along with the rest, and along with the racket, in the direction of the fire.

The fire was big. Not massive, not as huge as they could be. The really big ones, which were lit on or about May 1st every year, out and away from the town, on a sacred hill, were often as much as 8 metres high and as broad at the base too. But this fire was large all the same. And certainly big enough for the deep circle of people forming around it to keep themselves quite a long way back from the heat.

Frode skirted around it, too. Before stopping beside a small stone building which sheltered a well.

"Don't blame you!" said a man, laughing, nearby. "If there's a fire, the well is the best place to be!"

Frode smiled back at the man. Watching him for a while as he, too, lifted a child up onto his shoulders to have a better view of the lighting of the fire.

"Frode!" A vaguely familiar voice took Frode's attention away from the man and his child.

"Lok?" he said.

"Good to see you, old friend".

Like Frode, Lok was an itinerant trader. Unlike Frode, however, he spent most of his time very much within the vicinity of Ostmar. Trading between the town, the coast and the smaller neighbouring villages.

"Come and sit!" said Frode, making a bit of space on the stone wall for Lok.

Lok came over, brandishing a stone flask of ale. One of Alle's by the look of it. He offered Frode a drink, Frode accepted and took a swig from the bottle, and then, with a whoosh and a roar, the fire suddenly took hold.

And everybody cheered.

Overheard, the sky was now blackening quite quickly. (It should be said, that although the sun does set, in Southern Sweden, in midsummer – unlike in the north, where it does not – it is still light enough, outdoors, at midnight, for us today to read a book or newspaper. But by autumn, even early autumn, the time of this story, things have already moved markedly back in the other direction. And by mid-winter, it is pitch black by mid-afternoon).

For a while, Frode and Lok sat, chatting, watching the fire burn brighter and brighter, drinking, and listening to the excited voices of the youngest in the huge crowd.

"I hear they are leaving tomorrow", said Lok.

Frode, who had been watching the jugglers, on the far side of the fire, who were, it had to be said, little more than shadowy figures from this distance, turned to look at his companion. "Who? Who is?"

"The traders. The merchants. This fair. That's what this celebration has been for".

"Oh, yes", replied Frode absent-mindedly. "I was there and, yes, their boats were largely loaded. Full. I suppose they want to get moving now, before the colder weather arrives. It makes good sense".

Lok nodded. "They are hoping to take the evening tide, tomorrow", he said. "But I hear they do plan to return. I understand they have been very happy with their business here. Well... we all have, to be honest. It has been a big lift for us all here, in terms of trade".

"Yes", said Frode. "Yes, I imagine it must have been".

Two or three men walked past, nearby, and Frode could tell from their clothes that they were men or maybe even merchants from the boats. He didn't recognise them. And it didn't seem that Blokk was among them. But, yes, definitely, and only a short distance away there, too, was Vetle, and his men Auder and Ivar.

Instinctively Frode hunched up a little.

He would have been happy to speak with the merchants, had he been so able, had he spoke their language, but he had no desire whatsoever to talk to Vetle or the others.

Over on the other side of the big fire, there was a sudden burst of laughter. Cheering too. And, although he could not see them clearly, because of the fire and the gathering dark, Frode could just about make out that Ebba and Gan were now performing their tricks to a delighted crowd.

And for a moment, he considered getting up and walking around the fire to see the performance. Which would also take him further away from Vetle.

"The verifier", a steely voice said, from behind him. "Or am I mistaken?"

Frode turned. And, sure enough, Vetle was standing there, drink in one hand, other hand outstretched to greet Frode.

"Yes, it is I", said Frode, rising and grasping the man's wrist. "You are not mistaken".

"I'm sorry though, I don't recall your name", said Vetle.

"Frode".

"Ah. Yes. Of course. Very well known".

For a moment, the two stood, a rather awkward silence filling the space between them.

"It's good entertainment tonight", said Vetle at last. "There's even another one of those ridiculous dwarfs, I hear. A woman. Clowning. I really should go and try and find that. It sounds incredibly funny".

"Yes", said Frode coolly. "Yes, I'm sure it must be".

Again silence between the two men descended. Though, from the other side of the big fire, where the crowds were now thickest, the sounds of music and songs had begun.

"You are leaving tomorrow, I understand?" said Frode.

"Yes", said Vetle. "Be glad to get underway". And with that, brusquely, he turned on his heels. Saying only, as he walked away, "It's been good business here".

Frode was glad to see the man go.

"I don't like him", said Lok, quietly.

"No", said Frode. "Me neither".

A short while later and the great fire seemed almost to sigh, as a large portion of it sank inwards and down onto itself.

All around, people sat. Talked. Quieter now. The sound almost that of a deep, low buzzing. Replacing the more raucous noise of the afternoon and earlier evening.

Smoke hung thickly in the air.

And in many places, the youngest were sleeping. Outdoors. Though some, judging by the smaller size of the crowd, had already been taken back home and to bed.

Frode wished Lok the best of things, and took himself away to where the venison, or at least the last remains of the venison, were still being cut up.

"I don't mind what I have", he said to the burly woman, who was doing her utmost to carve every remaining fragment of meat from the animal. "A piece for now. And a piece for the morning, if possible. I have a journey to make on behalf of the town".

"Aye! No problems, there, my young man", said the woman. Deftly presenting Frode with two rather scraggy, but nevertheless chunky pieces of the meat.

Frode thanked her for them.

Took a few bites from one of the pieces of venison.

Took a few steps towards the fire.

But then he stopped.

Because there, just there, beside the fire, and to his huge surprise, he could see Ebba and Gan, talking to Vetle and his two comrades. Talking and even having a good laugh with them.

The sight jarred. It didn't make sense.

And Frode stepped back a little, away from the firelight.

Yes. There was no mistaking it. Ebba and Gan seemed to be on very good terms with Vetle. And they were even, or at least Ebba was, serving the three men some food. Stew or similar, from a small iron pot.

Frode shook his head. What on earth was that about?

"Ah! Here you are!" it was Alle. And the same two women. "We've been looking all over for you. Ran out of drink hours ago and now I feel stone sober. Well... a bit. More or less".

Frode tried to see what Ebba and Gan were doing. But a half dozen people now stood in the way, blocking his view.

"Now come on", said Alle. "I've a partner here for a dance, and a long story, and you've got to help me... two girls is one too many for an old fella like me".

The people moved.

Frode's view was no longer obscured.

But Ebba and Gan had gone.

"Come on!", said Alle. "Come!"

One of the young women took Frode by the arm. "Let's go and find some music", she said.

*

Morning arrived with a fine hangover.

Early start.

Pale light.

The fire had burned right down, but still smouldered, still gave off smoke.

And all around the embers, in fact everywhere in the town, people lay either asleep, half-asleep or slowly waking.

It looked, for all the world, as if the entire population had been mown down with a machine gun. Only, of course, this was the Iron Age, there were no machine guns, and people had simply fallen asleep, in rag-tag groups, after a great open-air party. A celebration of trade. Trade as it could be, bringing wealth to everyone and not just a few. Trade as it should be.

Frode stumbled, more or less, across, over and passing various people until he reached the well. There he drew up some water, plunged his face into the refreshing stuff, and emptied more of it over his head.

It had been a good night.

But the best way to clear a hangover was to get up, and get moving. And that was precisely what Frode did.

Within minutes, saying a few tired, headachy good mornings to people on the way, he walked out through the main gate, heading for the hut where the Crone lived.

The walk would take an hour.

No more.

The tracks from Ostmar, divided down, one by one, until Frode found himself on what was no more than a very narrow footpath – narrow and scarcely used because few people, and even those few but rarely, dared visit the hut of the Crone.

It wasn't that her 'magic' was poor. Quite the opposite. Everybody, for a distance around, knew that the Crone could heal almost every sickness. Or so it appeared. And, more than that, it was also firmly held that she had direct access to the dead. For her own gain or, if she chose it, for the gain of others. So she was both well known and widely-respected.

But she was also considered to be a woman not to cross. And most certainly a woman to avoid. After all, with such powers, what was to prevent her from harming a visitor or even putting the evil eye on them?

A deer suddenly ran out in front of Frode.

A big one, wild.

It ran straight out, onto the path. Stopped. Turned. Stared for want of a better word at Frode, challenging almost, then fleet-footed it disappeared back in the densely overgrown woodland.

The appearance of the animal had made Frode start.

"Thankyou", he said. "That helped me wake up. And given where I am going, it's probably just as well I have my wits about me on this fine morning".

He made the Iron Age equivalent of the sign of the cross, looked skywards once, then resumed his journey.

And within a few minutes he had arrived.

The Crone lived in a hut that had seen better days. It was, rather like Ebba's home, weathered grey wood, patched up in places with new planks or even, here and there, with dollops of mud or dung. Or both.

The roof, of straw, was thin and did not look as if it kept any of the elements out. Neither sun nor rain.

Despite those similarities, to countless other poor and isolated dwellings, however, the hut of the crone had one notable exception; it had been built upon what was once a pond. And which, occasionally, still became one, if the rains were excessive.

As a result of that, the hut stood on what could only be described as stilts. And it was reached, in a similar manner to which the ships had been reached, via a raised wooden walkway. Numerous narrow planks of which, needless to say, were missing.

Fortunately, the day was still, the pond below was dry and the drop, should that happen, was not too far.

But Frode wondered, as he began to cross the dilapidated bridge, quite how the thing would feel in an almost horizontal snow storm. The likes of which blew often, in winter, across the plains of southern Sweden.

"Hello", he called, as he reached mid-point in the walkway. Not truly comfortable going any further and hoping a response would prevent that need. "Per? Crone? Are you there? Anybody?"

Calling the woman 'crone' may have seemed rather rude. But it was the woman herself who chose to be known by that name. No doubt, in part, to enhance her sinister reputation. And it didn't do to go against her wishes.

Frode waited.

Called again.

And then, quite abruptly, a face appeared in the low, dark, doorway of the hut. Directly ahead of Frode.

"Per!"

And it was, indeed, the little man. The missing sculptor from Ostmar.

"Frode!" Per called the name with some joy. And, to the delight of Frode, he scrambled out of the dank looking hut, without any apparent sign of ill-health.

"Per! My little man!", said Frode, taking a few uneasy steps forwards. "How good it is to see you. How good it is!"

The two men met on the walkway and, forgetting all formality, simply embraced. Each, it seemed, equally delighted to see the other.

"What times are these?" said Frode, stepping back to look at Per. "The troubles you have given me".

Both men laughed.

"I know", said Per. "Ebba has told me all about it. Until yesterday I was either asleep, near death or as vague as a mist on a hot summers day. But yesterday morning, thanks to the crone, I awoke feeling both hungry and well".

Frode, exaggeratedly, glanced left and right. Behind and in front. "And the crone?" he whispered. "Is she here? Is she around?"

Per shook his head. "No, no. She is away, as I believe she is most days. Collecting herbs or casting spells. Who can say? It is only the evening, I gather, that she spends here, in this... rather forbidding place of hers".

Frode looked past Per at the Crone's hut. It did not, in any way, look an inviting sort of spot to sit and talk.

"Are you well enough to walk a little?" said Frode. "Off this bridge before it snaps. Perhaps we can we find a sunlit place to sit a while, for I think we need to talk".

"Yes", said Per, for all the world looking as if he had never had a day's illness in his life. "Yes. Lead on. I can follow. I am quite well".

The two men came uneasily off the walkway, walked a short distance away from the gloomy hut of the crone, and sat down on a few low, rounded boulders, in a place where the honest sunshine fell on both of their faces.

"So then", began Frode...

10

"I know you were here, resting here, and almost dying here. You were here to be brought back to health. And it looks to have worked", said Frode. "And I also understand that it was only yesterday morning, in any meaningful sense, that you recovered consciousness. You could talk, think. All of that".

"Yes", said Per. "That is pretty much true. Apparently, on and off, I have rambled a bit, you know, like when a person talks in their sleep. That kind of thing. But nothing, as far I can tell, that made any sense".

Frode nodded. "Yes. I've seen many ill people do that. But it is often a good sign, that they are still with us and on the mend".

"And here I am", said Per, with a quick smile. "Mended. I hope".

"You know too, I assume, from Ebba if not from the Crone, that you were suspected of murder. That the elders of Ostmar had sent men out to find you, to bring you back for trial".

Per frowned. "Yes. I believe that is true. It feels very strange to know that has been going on, all whilst I was oblivious to the world". He paused. Looked hard at Frode. "And you, my friend, had been summoned here as verifier, to investigate that very charge?"

"Indeed I was", said Frode.

For a moment neither man spoke. And it was Frode who broke the silence. "You know, we both know, of course, that you did not kill the man who came into your hut that night. The man who attacked you. The man who almost, so it seems, killed you".

Per studied Frode's face carefully as he spoke those words. Evidently, it seemed to Frode, trying to see if Frode was guessing or making a statement of fact. Unsure, perhaps, how much Frode knew. Unsure, perhaps, of what he had and what he had not yet discovered.

"I did not kill him", said Per. His words almost a question.

"No", said Frode firmly. "You did not. I was brought to Ostmar to see if a murder had taken place and to discover if you were the murderer. I find neither thing has happened. I find that your apprentice, Suli, killed the man. And that he did it, in effect, to save your life. So there was no crime. It was a clear matter of self-defence".

"Ah", said Per. Visibly relieved, or at least so it seemed to Frode, that the truth was now out.

"Ah, indeed", said Frode. "And I have reported as much back to the elders at Ostmar".

"Ebba told me that", said Per slowly, "More or less. Though I was still rather groggy when she did so. So to hear the news from your own lips serves me much better. Thankyou".

Frode said nothing.

Per sighed. A heavy sigh. "I suppose I would be more glad of it, of being found innocent, had I some recollection of the thing", he said at last. "But from the night of the attack until yesterday, I remember nothing. Though that is not to say I am ungrateful for what you have done. Quite the opposite".

"It is my duty to discover the truth", said Frode. "So now you can return home. And resume your life".

"Yes", said Per. "Yes, I can".

It was obvious to both men, from the way they spoke, that there was more to come. Frode was not here simply to tell Per he could go back home. And Per was old enough and wise enough to realise that the rest of the story, the truth of the story, would now have to come out.

"You want to know what happened", said Per. The words spoken quietly. "Who the man was".

"Yes", said Frode. "Not for the elders, you understand. As far as they are concerned, you are a free man. But for myself, and for you, for us as friends. For the sake of friendship. You see, you ran away that night, and you left Suli behind to lie for you. Which the boy did. Which he did very well. So strongly did that lad stand by you, in fact, that you were suspected of murder. It was his word that stood against you".

"Yes", said Per quietly. "I know".

"I can understand your running", said Frode. "For that, I hold nothing against you. But to put Suli in that position? Why? And how could you do that? Why not simply confess the truth? You were attacked. Suli defended you. Killed the man. Why did you bring the blame onto yourself through Suli? That much, I cannot yet understand".

Per took a long, slow, deep breath. Wanting to answer. But not yet able to do so. Simply shaking his head instead.

"Somehow", continued Frode, "I think you were trying to protect him? That is what he says. But now I need you to tell me that is so. And also, in a way, you did that to protect yourself? But if so, then how and from whom?"

Per stood. Took a few paces away from Frode.

Shook his head.

Turned. Came back.

Years and years the secret he had kept. And it was not easy to bring it out. To tell somebody about it. But now, he knew, he needed to do so. For his own sake, for peace of mind, and for the sake of this friendship.

"Like you, I came from the far north", said Per at last, sitting down once more, staring at the ground as he spoke. "Life, like the weather, is harder up there. Sometimes brutal. My village, when I was about the same age as Suli is now, was sacked by marauders. Mercenaries. The winter had arrived early. People were starving. And a nearby warlord had hired these men to get food for him, using any and all means they wanted". He paused. Looked Frode in the face. In the eyes. "So they arrived one evening, in the deep snow, and they slaughtered everybody in my village. Hacking, killing, burning, raping. Destroying. It was a scene from hell itself. Nothing and no one was spared. No one except for me. Three times I dodged out from under their swords, those evil men, their faces glowering down at me. Laughing. Yet I escaped, out into the wild forest. Just me. With the sights and screams of my village ringing in my ears. I tried to help... I wanted to help... but I could do nothing".

He looked back down at the floor again. Drew a deep breath. Then Per resumed his tale. "I was half dead in that forest, in the snow. I have no idea to this day who found me, but one morning, rather like now, I awoke in a village, and there I was. Alive. Safe. But with the horrors of that night fixed forever in my mind".

"From there, after a time, I moved south. As far south as I could manage. To put as much distance between myself, that warlord and his murderous hirelings as possible".

"You came to Ostmar", said Frode.

"Yes, eventually", said Per. "And from the day I arrived until the other night, I buried myself in my work there. I lived for it. For my work. And for nothing else. Because as soon as I stopped working, the images of that night came back".

Frode nodded. In truth there was little he could say. Little he could add.

Per continued, "As Suli would avow, regularly, I slept and saw that sacking all over again. In my dreams. A nightmare. Waking from it scared, terrified. In the middle of the night. Horrors. So many times. So very many times".

"You've told Suli all of this?"

"No", said Per. "I pretended it was just a dream. A recurring dream. But no, I've never told anyone any of this. Not until yesterday morning, when I told Ebba. For she asked me much the same questions as you have asked me. Why? Why did I not just claim self-defence? Why ask Suli to lie on my behalf? So you are the only other person who knows. Who must ever know".

At those last words, Per's expression changed. Fear, an almost animal fear, appeared in his face. His eyes, widening, whitening, as if remembering the men, the murders and that night in his own home. As if, perhaps, dreading more of the same at some point in the future.

Frode had guessed the rest. But now, at last, he was certain of it. "That man", he said. "Was he one of those mercenaries? Is that the fear you have?"

Per slowly nodded his head. "Yes. Yes", he said. "The traders arrived one morning. From overseas. Good men. Honest merchants. But with them... came some of our own people".

"Yes", said Frode, "Yes, I have met them. There are or there were four of them... wait, what? Do you mean that all four of them were mercenaries?"

Again Per nodded his head. Slowly. "I was at the town gate, when they first came to Ostmar. Came there with some of the traders. I recognised them immediately. Those are the faces of my nightmares. Years and years of nightmares. They are not faces I would easily forget".

"And they recognised you, too?"

"Yes", said Per. He hesitated, and then pointed at himself. "Had I been as other men, in stature, I am sure they would not have known me. But as I saw them, so they saw me. At least their leader saw me".

Per shook his head. As it trying to remove the horrible memory of that meeting.

"I went home. Afeared. I knew they had seen me and I felt sure they recognised me. But then, as the hours passed, I told myself no. I made myself calm down. To them, I was nothing. An object of derision. That was what I told myself. And so I tried to get back on with my life...".

"Until one of them, presumably trying to silence you, crashed into your home an evening or two later?"

"Yes", said Per. "Exactly that, exactly that. The man came into my home, and tried to kill me. As you say, I am sure they were afraid I would tell the elders who they were and what they were. And they had decided to silence me. And they nearly succeeded too".

"But they did not know that Suli was also in your home. Asleep on the floor, almost invisible, beneath a great pile of straw".

Per nodded. "Yes. That must have been it. They had no idea he was there. And the boy... that boy... Suli, he saved my life".

Frode frowned. Considered the story a moment.

The sound of birds singing in the trees around where they sat, the feel of the sun, seemed to be a long way from the horrors which Per had just described.

"One man dead", said Frode slowly. "Three more to go... At that moment, as the man fell dead in your hut, you were very quick witted".

"Yes, that is true", said Per. "I saw immediately that if I ran, and had the blame placed on me for the killing, then the others would not harm Suli, because he would be witness against me, not against them. Nor would they feel the need to pursue me, either, because I would surely die for having killed their accomplice. On condition that I took the blame, and Suli was my accuser, justice would have accounted for me. Those evil men would go about their business and soon enough leave these shores and go back to their new homelands".

Frode nodded slowly. It all made sense.

And it made good sense, too.

It was incredibly quick thinking on Per's part, and selfless. By taking the blame for the murder, not only was he giving himself a chance but he was, in effect, also protecting Suli.

And from what Frode had known, ever known, about Per, that gamble fitted the man. The man he was still proud to call a friend.

Frode stood.

It was time to go.

Per was tiring. He needed rest. And Frode had to go back to Ostmar.

The two men embraced again.

And each turned to leave.

"Oh, but what if the elders *had* found you?" said Frode, asking one last question of Per. "You would have been tried for murder."

"I know", said Per. "But if that had happened, I would have stood by my story anyway. I would have preferred to die that way, under their justice, than for those evil men to return and get their hands on me".

*

Walking back through the early autumn woods, walking in the direction of Ostmar, the tracks slowly merging, becoming wider and gradually busier, with a pale blue sky overhead, and a light wind ruffling the leaves of the trees as he passed them by, Frode felt rather pleased with himself.

Or, more accurately, rather pleased with life.

He had done his duty. He had found that Per, a friend, was innocent of murder.

But more than that, he had gone to see Per, to answer – for the sake of that friendship more than anything else – one or two outstanding but important questions. And the answers which Per had given him to those questions, not only made good sense, but helped, in a way, restore his faith in human kind.

Yes, there was no shortage of evil in the world. Men like Vetle and the others. But so long as there were people like Per, people who would think clearly and do the right thing, and act out of friendship for others rather than simply put themselves first, then there was always hope for the world.

That thought made Frode smile.

And that smile broadened as a young man, with a very young child, both probably having been at the festival in

Ostmar, the night before, passed Frode and bid him a good day.

Yes, life could be good.

Per would move back to town. Resume his life. And even, quite probably, receive some sort of admiration for having fought off a killer in the night.

Suli too. The quiet boy had begun to grow into a man.

It was good. It was all good.

Only...

There was something else. There was something missing. Something small, a concern, a doubt, a worry, inside Frode. Something perhaps triggered by his years of experience as a verifier.

Per would go home. Yes.

Those men would leave. Yes.

But they would also come back.

Trade had been good. So they would assuredly come back.

Instinctively, as that thought struck him, Frode changed direction. There was something else. It was no more than a hunch, a feeling, an idea. But he needed to look into it. And so, with the smile now gone from his face, he headed, as quickly as he could, to Ebba's home. Turning off the track to Ostmar and, after losing his way a little, finding the narrow path which led to her weather-worn hut.

Last night, at the fair, Ebba and Gan had been laughing and joking with Vetle, Auder and Ivar. The killers. Mercenaries. Call them what you will.

Last night that had been.

And yet it had been early that same morning, that Per had told Ebba his story.

Why, then, was she talking to them? Joking with them?

Frode reached Ebba's poor little home, just in time to see the diminutive woman coming back from a quick visit to her garden. To the far side of her garden. Answering the call of nature.

"Ebba!" he called. "You are here".

The sight of Ebba, briefly, brought that smile back to Frode's face.

Certainly some part of him, some part deep inside no doubt, had been worried that Vetle and the others may have harmed her. But no. She was here. And she seemed to be well.

"Yes!" Ebba called back, "Of course I am here. Where else would I be?"

"Oh, I don't know", said Frode, a little out of breath, from rushing to see her. "I... I sort of lost sight of you last night, at the festival", he lied. "And I guess I was just a bit surprised to see you back here. Erm... so soon, I mean".

Ebba shrugged. "It's not so early. And, in any case, Gan and I left town during the night. We know our way back home, even in the dark". She frowned at Frode. Saw the worry in his face. "Are you alright?"

"Yes", said Frode. "Yes. I'm fine. Just... just a bit out of breath. Well... no. No, that's not quite true. And to tell you the truth, I was a little concerned, a bit worried about you".

Ebba frowned. "You were? Worried about me? Why?"

"Well", said Frode, "To be honest, I have just come from Per, from talking to him".

"Ah", said Ebba. "I see. And how is he today? Better, I trust?"

"Yes", said Frode. "Yes. He is very well. In fact he is hoping to return home within a few days".

"To Ostmar?"

"Yes".

"That is wonderful news", said Ebba. "So do you want to come in, for a while, rest, drink or eat? Are you tired?"

"Erm... no", said Frode. "Thankyou but no. I have to get on my way, to Ostmar. Speak to the elders. Put the last few things to bed, as it were. So that everyone can get back on with their lives again".

"Oh, that is good", said Ebba. "Then I shall not detain you. I have food to prepare for Gan, he is cutting firewood for me, for the cold days ahead. In return, I make sure he is well fed. He has a very good appetite, you know!"

Frode laughed. "I can well imagine that".

Ebba turned to go in. A small bunch of greenery in her hand. Some flavouring for Gan's dinner, perhaps.

"Ebba?"

"Yes".

Even though he already knew the answer to the question, Frode asked it anyway. "Did Per tell you... about the man, the dead man? I mean, who he was".

Ebba, a long time wary, glanced left and right. But there was nobody about. She nodded. "Yes. He told me".

"Yesterday? He told you yesterday, when you went to see him in the morning?"

Again Ebba nodded. "Yes".

"And he told you... everything?"

"Yes", said Ebba. "And you? He has also told you, then? About the nightmares, and his home village. All of it?"

"Yes", said Frode.

Ebba shook her head. "The poor wee man", she said. "To think, all of those years he had been living with that horror inside of him. Never telling another soul".

The sound of a grand pile of wood being dropped onto the ground and the approach of heavier than normal footsteps, suggested the return of Gan.

"Those evil, evil men", said Ebba. "And to think they were here, too. In our midst".

"Yes", said Frode. Something inside him felt almost tangible, there was a sense of alarm, an instinct, a worry, something beyond words, that same thing which so many years ago had marked him out to be a verifier. "So... so then is Per not *still* in danger from those men?"

Ebba frowned, then simply shook her head and laughed.

"Because their ships sail this evening?" said Frode. "But you must know they will return. Trade here was very good. They will return".

"Not they", said Ebba, her tone quite definite. "Not those men. It would be good news for all of us if the merchants return, yes. But those evil men will never come back".

Gan appeared around the corner of the house. Saw Frode and grunted a greeting of a kind.

Frode smiled back at the gentle giant.

"Per told me his story in the house of the Crone. She was there too, and she heard it all and, may the gods bless her, she was more than willing to help me prepare the meal which those same men ate, last night, at the festival".

So *that* was what Ebba was doing. "I saw you", said Frode. Surprise evident in his voice. "You and Gan. Talking to those men".

"Talking to them? Oh, yes", said Ebba. "Talking to them, chatting away as friendly as we could be, and all the while making sure they ate a very special stew, too. And plenty of it. Plenty of it for each of them".

"A special stew?"

Ebba nodded. "It is autumn. And what better flavouring for a stew than fresh, wild mushrooms". She turned to look at Gan. "There is some bread inside", she said to the big man. "Dinner will be a while yet".

Gan smiled and went into the little hut. Lowering his head slightly as went through the doorway.

"Mushrooms?" said Frode, wanting to prevent it, but being quite unable to stop a huge smile from spreading across his face.

"Yes", said Ebba. "And you can take it from me that not one of those three men will ever see their adopted homelands again. Which, of course, also means that Per may now go home safely. He has nothing more to fear from any of them".

She briskly rubbed her hands together, took a deep breath of the fresh, crisp air and gave Frode a broad grin.

"Now, I really must get Gan his dinner, he works so hard and eats so much".

Sometimes, it felt to Frode, as he bid Ebba farewell and set off once more for Ostmar, justice could take a long time to arrive. But arrive it usually did. Almost invariably did. Albeit, as in this case, from the most unexpected of sources.

FIN

For those who would like to know a tiny bit more... the following extract is taken from Wikipedia

Amanita virosa, commonly known in Europe as the **destroying angel** or the **European destroying angel**, is a deadly poisonous fungus, one of many in the genus Amanita.

Immature specimens resemble several edible species commonly consumed by humans, increasing the risk of accidental poisoning. <u>Just one single cap of *Amanita virosa* is enough to kill an adult human</u>.

What makes these mushrooms so dangerous?

Although causing many fatalities this deadly fungus has no known antidote. The symptoms start several hours after ingestion with severe vomiting, diarrhoea and abdominal pains and can last for several days; this is followed by what seems to be a full recovery... this soon lapses, and ends in death from kidney and liver failure.

More books from the same author:

FRODE: Iron Age detective

OUT SOON - Murder at Brae

FRODE is a trader in amber, and he is travelling to the coast to take advantage of recent storms which often was that precious material ashore.

BUT there has been a DEATH in the nearby village of Brae, and once he is summoned by the mysterious 'Whistlers', Frode has no choice but to go along and investigate...

OUT NOW - A YEAR in KRONOBERG: It's in SWEDEN

In the same style as Peter Mayle's "A Year in Provence", two Brits move to SWEDEN and set up a new home there.

This is a tale about snow, more snow, and long hot summer days.

BUT it's also a story about a gate, helpful neighbours, Eurovision, mosquitoes, a drunken moose, ice, blizzards and an angry squirrel...

Printed in Great Britain
by Amazon